WANDERVILLE

On Track for Treasure

WENDY McCLURE

WANDERVILLE

On Track for Treasure

razor
bill

An Imprint of Penguin Group (USA)

razOr
bill

Penguin.com
Razorbill, an Imprint of Penguin Random House

Copyright © 2014 Penguin Group (USA), LLC

Library of Congress Cataloging-in-Publication Data

McClure, Wendy.
  On track for treasure / Wendy McClure.
    pages cm. -- (Wanderville ; 2)
  Summary: "When the town sheriff discovers the exact location of 'Wanderville,' the orphans who live there--Jack, Frances, Harold, Alexander, and their new friends--must flee their home in the woods"-- Provided by publisher.
  ISBN 978-1-59514-703-5 (paperback)
  [1. Orphans--Fiction 2. Homeless persons--Fiction. 3. Adventure and adventurers--Fiction. 4. Brothers and sisters--Fiction.] I. Title.
  PZ7.M4784141947On 2014
  [Fic]--dc23

                              2014026996

Printed in the United States of America

 1 3 5 7 9 10 8 6 4 2

Interior design by Eric Ford

For Claire, Kate,
Kelly, and Molly.

Shine on!

1

WAITING FOR THE SIGNAL

Whitmore, Kansas

They were going to miss the train. Jack was sure of it.

"Where'd Alexander go?" Frances whispered.

She was right next to Jack, but the boys' cap she was wearing was shoved down so low on her forehead that Jack wondered how she could see at all. Somehow, though, she and her kid brother, Harold, had managed to stay close behind Jack as they dashed through town from one backyard to another. Now the three of them pressed themselves against the wall of a shed just off Third Street, hoping the narrow strip of shade under the eaves would be enough to conceal them. It was a good thing the other kids were waiting in the empty stable a block away—they would never all fit in this spot.

Compared with the Lower East Side of New York, where Jack was from, Whitmore, Kansas, was just a sleepy hamlet. Yet nothing Jack had ever experienced in the dim and teeming alleys of Manhattan—not even at night—could match the panic he felt now, in the brightest noon daylight, in this tiny town just five blocks long. There was nowhere to hide in a place like this—and certainly nowhere *ten* runaways could hide. Except, that is, on the next train west. Alexander had said it was their only chance.

Jack's mind flashed back to that morning, when Sheriff Routh had found the clearing in the woods where they'd been living—the place they called Wanderville. It had been the only real home they'd known since leaving New York. They'd been on an orphan train, which took poor kids out of the cities and sent them west. But rather than live with strangers, Jack, Frances, and Harold had escaped. Wanderville wasn't just a home, but a town all their own, a safe place. They'd also rescued other orphan train kids, who'd been forced to work at the Pratcherd ranch nearby. Just that morning, in fact, one more had come to Wanderville: Quentin.

But then the sheriff had shown up, too. The kids had gotten away before he could round them up, but if they didn't get out of town on the next train, he would catch up to them. And this time he would have the Pratcherds with him, because it was clear he was on *their* side now.

"Do you see Alexander?" Frances asked again.

"Not yet," Jack whispered. "Just wait. He'll give the signal soon."

Where was *Alexander?* he wondered. Alexander, who had been one of the first ones to come out here on an orphan train, knew the area better than anyone, so he'd run ahead to make sure all was clear by the train tracks. He was supposed to come by the corner of the livery barn and signal that it was safe to make a run for it. But he hadn't shown up so far, and time was running out.

"I can hear the train—" Harold began, his voice too loud, but Frances clapped a hand over his mouth to hush him.

The kid was right: The train had come in, and it was waiting up by the depot, just out of sight, beyond the buildings on Front Street. They could hear it chuffing and hissing, standing idle—for the moment at least.

"Come *on*," Jack heard Frances mutter under her breath. She, too, was staring hard at the spot where their friend was supposed to appear. They could see past the livery barn to the train tracks glinting in the sun.

If they waited any longer, Jack knew, they'd soon see the train passing by, and with it their best chance of getting out of town fast. He didn't even *want* to get on that train, but they couldn't go back into the woods. By now, Jack was sure, the sheriff and the Pratcherds were storming into Wanderville on horseback. Sheriff Routh himself was probably tearing down the hammocks they'd slept in, kicking aside the rocks around the fireplace, destroying everything they'd built. . . .

But Jack couldn't let himself think about that now. "We should get the others," he said. "They're waiting over in the stable, right?"

"Yes, but—" Frances suddenly stopped. She pushed her hat back, and Jack could see her eyes were wide.

Then he heard them, too: footsteps. Slow ones, as if they were sneaking up, coming around the side of the lean-to.

He mouthed the words to Frances: *The sheriff.*

Frances nodded and mouthed back: *Let's go.* She grabbed Harold's arm.

Then someone grabbed *Jack*'s arm.

"*Hey!*" he yelped.

"Hey yourself!" a familiar voice whispered.

It wasn't the sheriff, though it was someone tall—Lorenzo, who had crept over with Sarah from the stable.

"We need to go!" Lorenzo insisted. He and Sarah had come out to Kansas on the same orphan train as Jack and Frances. They hadn't worked long at the Pratcherd ranch, but like the rest of them, they never wanted to go back there—Jack could tell from their anxious faces.

"We can hear the train!" Sarah sounded frantic, and she kept trying to tuck her braids up inside her hat.

After they left Wanderville that morning, some of the kids had tried to disguise themselves in case they ran into the Pratcherds in town. The boys shook dust into their hair to dull their hair color—for Harold, who had bright red hair, this was especially necessary—and the girls hid their hair under caps and hats. Frances even donned an old pair of breeches so that she'd be taken for a boy.

But none of these measures would do them a lick of good if Sheriff Routh caught them.

There was no more time to wait. "Let's go!" Jack said, his voice suddenly hoarse. "Lorenzo, get the others and then follow me. The rest of you"—he looked over at Frances and Harold and Sarah— "run for the tracks. *Now!*"

Sarah dashed out first, and then Frances raced across Front Street with Harold, the wind roaring in her ears. *Don't look back,* she thought. If anyone had spotted them and was giving chase, she didn't want to know. She held on tight to Harold's hand, and together they darted around the corner of the livery barn.

There was the train, stopped just a little ways down the tracks. And then, over the noise of the wind, the train's whistle, long and mournful. It was about to leave.

She and Harold ran faster, catching up with Sarah, their shoes kicking up gravel and cinders. They were just reaching the train's caboose when she saw Alexander, waving his arms wildly. He was leaning out the doorway of one of the freight cars near the back. He motioned frantically to Frances and Harold and Sarah: *Over here!*

"Get in first," she whispered to Harold as she helped him climb up into the empty boxcar and wriggle inside. He was just seven but strangely heavy all of a sudden. Then she gave Sarah a hand; and soon Lorenzo came with Anka and little George—two more kids they'd rescued from the Pratcherds—and she helped them crawl in, too.

The next thing she knew, the train's whistle was blowing again, right over their heads, and Jack was there with Nicky and Quentin, all of them clambering up the ladder rails and heaving themselves over the threshold of the freight car. She looked behind her—was anyone else coming?

But there was only the dusty end of Front Street, looking remarkably still under the noontime glare. Even the depot was empty. She felt an odd swooning sensation. No, it was the train, starting to move, and she was still on the ground, standing beside it.

"Frances! Grab the *ladder*!" Nicky was calling to her. "Get on the ladder!" He meant the ladder that went up the side of the car next to the door. Frances grabbed the highest rung she could and hauled her feet up. But she didn't know how she'd get across to reach the door. It had looked easy when the other kids climbed into the car, but the train hadn't been moving then. She tried to swing. . . .

Suddenly, an arm reached out and grabbed her by the belt of her breeches. A *big* arm, like a tree branch, and she was yanked inside.

"Almost missed the train, kid," spoke a low and gravelly voice. It was dim inside the freight car, and she couldn't make out the face of her rescuer. Whoever he was, he sounded a thousand years old.

As her eyes adjusted, Frances could see the other children sitting on the floor nearby. Her legs felt weak, and when she plopped down beside Sarah and Harold, a wave of relief washed over her.

"Th-thank you," she said.

"You're quite welcome," the thousand-year-old voice replied. Frances could see that the man had a long coat and a bundle tied to one shoulder. *A hobo!* she realized. She'd heard stories about the hoboes, or bindle stiffs—the tramps who rode the rails. But she hadn't known whether they were real or just a legend. Now she knew.

The hobo tipped his hat to the children and

smiled—a kind smile, though with teeth the color of tenement bricks. "Where might you and your small-ish companions be headed?" he asked Frances.

She was still too stunned to speak.

But Harold answered for her. "California!"

2
WHAT CAME BEFORE

The train was picking up speed. The freight car bumped and swayed in a way the passenger cars never had on the trip from New York. Frances recalled that during that ride her stomach had felt all twisted up, too, though for much different reasons.

"If you will excuse me," said the hobo, "much as I enjoy conversating about California, I got a reserved seat over thataways."

Frances and Harold watched as he shuffled over to the far end of the car without ever losing his balance, even as everything jostled and bucked around him. *I'd like to see Miss DeHaven try that*, Frances thought, remembering the mean, elegantly dressed orphan train chaperone who'd clearly despised them, and how she could stand perfectly motionless in the train aisle like a dreadful apparition.

Frances shook off the memory. Now she watched as the hobo plunked down next to a pile of dusty clothing, which, on second glance, appeared to be another fellow, curled up, asleep. Then the first hobo leaned back against the side of the car and began to doze off, too.

She looked around the dim car. Besides the children, the only other passengers were the two vagabonds. No cargo at all, just some scattered straw and a few odds and ends that rattled over the scuffed floor—the lid of a tobacco tin, an old shoe. Miss DeHaven would hate this place even more than she did children, Frances realized with some satisfaction.

She turned to tell Jack. But he was in the corner with Alexander, and the two were having an intense discussion, their voices low. No, not a discussion—an argument.

"You were supposed to give the signal!" Jack hissed.

"And *you* were supposed to *wait*," Alexander shot back. "But you didn't!"

"Wait until when? The train was leaving!"

"I knew what I was doing, Jack! I had to make sure the sheriff wasn't around."

"Look, leaving town was *your* idea, not mine, but I wasn't going to wait around until we all got caught. . . ."

Frances had to bite her lip to keep from yelling at them both. Had they even noticed how a *hobo* had saved her from falling off the side of the train and breaking her neck? But there was no use in making a scene in front of everyone else. She crept over to the boys.

"Hey." She nudged Jack, who fell quiet. So did Alexander. "Shouldn't we do a head count? Make sure everyone's here?"

"Good idea," Alexander said.

"Better than ones *you've* had," Jack muttered under his breath.

Frances pretended not to hear him as she began to count. "There's the three of us, and then Harold, which makes four. And then Lorenzo . . ." She nodded at the dark-haired tall boy. "And Sarah and Anka." The two girls looked up at the sound of their names. Sarah was smoothing her braids, and shy blond Anka, who spoke only a little English, had taken off her hat. "That makes seven," Frances continued. "Plus Nicky and George, right?"

"And Quentin," Jack pointed out. "Quentin makes ten of us now. Don't forget him."

Quentin had joined them shortly before they left Wanderville. Now he sat by himself near the center of the car, fidgeting idly with some straw he'd picked up.

Frances counted him, too. How could she have overlooked Quentin? He was the reason they were on this train.

Quentin hung his head as he fidgeted, and Jack could see that he felt bad about all that had happened.

Jack's mind went back to the past couple of weeks. Alexander, Frances, Harold, and Jack had been the first citizens of Wanderville, the town they'd created in a wooded ravine as a place where kids could be safe—especially kids who'd come west on the orphan trains like they had and who'd decided to run away rather than be sent off with strangers who would force them to work like dogs.

They'd set up hammocks for sleeping, and a place to cook, and there was a little creek that ran through the ravine where they could get water. Sometimes they'd sneak into Whitmore to find food—Alexander was especially good at "liberating" tinned goods from the mercantile and eggs from the henhouses—and before long they had enough supplies to live very well on their own.

Eventually, Jack and his friends helped five more escape from the Pratcherd ranch: Nicky, Lorenzo, George, Anka, and Sarah. But there were still more than a dozen orphan train children toiling as farmhands there. Quentin was one of them, and Jack was determined to go back to the ranch to free him.

In fact, Jack wanted to rescue every kid he could, and only his closest friends, Frances and Alexander, knew the deep-down reason why. It was because of Daniel. Daniel, his brother, who had died in a factory fire back in New York, and who Jack hadn't been able to save.

So they all began to carry out their plan to bring the rest of the children to Wanderville. At first, everything went smoothly:

Sarah and Lorenzo crept through a field to the edge of the ranch and discovered a hole in the far fence.

Then Anka, who had an excellent sense of

direction, drew a map that showed how to escape through the fence hole and get to Wanderville.

Jack added a set of instructions for Quentin and the other farmhands to follow. *Wait until Friday, then go out after midnight. Cross the last field on the map, and we will meet you by the lone tree.*

From their spying they'd figured out that Mr. Pratcherd left town on supply runs on Friday and came back Saturday afternoon, leaving only Mrs. Pratcherd and her son, Rutherford. They were bad enough, but at least there'd be one less Pratcherd to worry about.

Finally, Jack and Alexander sneaked over to Whitmore, where they found Rutherford Pratcherd's shiny buggy parked outside the gun shop. Jack kept watch while Alexander slipped out and tied the note and map to a spoke on one of the rear wheels. They were going off advice from Nicky, who had remembered how Rutherford would make the farmhands wash the buggy wheels every day to keep them "clean as china plates." Quentin had to do chores for Rutherford all the time, so Jack hoped that he would be the one to find the note.

"Fingers crossed," Alexander said as they watched the buggy drive off. "Now we wait until Friday."

But they didn't make it to Friday. The very next morning, just after dawn, Jack and the others were awakened by the sound of dogs barking.

"They sound like they're chasing someone!" Frances said.

Then came the patter of footsteps. One person, running, then crashing through the bushes near the top of the ravine and stumbling down into the woods.

Alexander was already on his feet, holding out his hatchet for defense. "Who's there?" he called.

"It's me!" gasped the intruder. "Quentin!"

Quentin was still struggling to catch his breath. Though Quentin's crooked front lip always made him look like he was sneering, Jack could tell he'd had quite a scare. The others gathered around, full of questions.

"Where are the rest of the kids?" Alexander demanded. "Did they escape with you?"

"N-no," Quentin panted. "Just me . . ."

"*What?*" Alexander was furious. "You just left on your own?"

"You did the same thing when *you* escaped from the ranch," Jack reminded him.

"No! Listen to me!" Quentin insisted. "I was just trying—"

"Trying to put us all in danger?" Frances interrupted. "What about those dogs out there?"

"I didn't *know* there'd be guard dogs!" Quentin cried. "But, I mean, I think I outran 'em."

Jack shook his head. "Those dogs probably woke up half the town of Whitmore, Quentin! What if it's not only the dogs that are chasing you? What if it's the Pratcherds, or . . ."

"Or the sheriff," Alexander said, his voice suddenly a whisper. His face had gone pale at the sight of something at the top of the ravine. Jack and the others turned to follow his gaze.

There, at the edge of the woods, was a man on horseback: Sheriff Routh. Jack could see the glint of his badge.

"So this is where you brats have been keeping yourselves," the sheriff said, smirking as he looked all around.

Nobody moved or spoke, but then Frances stepped in front of her little brother, Harold, as if to protect him. "It's better than the bunker at that wretched ranch!" she called out. "Better than being forced to dig all day in those fields. Why don't you let us be?"

The sheriff's eyes narrowed at Frances. "I don't

care anymore how rough you had it out there. You little worms tried to make a monkey of me the day you stole that wagon from the Pratcherds," he said. "And they will be very interested to know where you are now." He pointed at Alexander. "Especially *you*."

Alexander was still pale, but he squared his shoulders. He had been the first one to escape from the Pratcherds, and it had been his idea to start Wanderville.

"Is that so?" Alexander said. Jack could hear a slight tremble in his words. But then Alexander took a breath and raised his voice. "I'd like to see you try to arrest all *ten* of us right now!"

"Yeah!" Frances called. "Just try it!"

The boys joined in as well. "Go ahead!" Quentin jeered.

But Jack held his tongue. The sheriff had a look about him that was different today: He glared at them all fiercely. The man seemed to be boiling inside, and suddenly Jack understood that this wasn't about breaking the law anymore. This was about revenge. They'd made the sheriff look foolish in the town of Whitmore.

"You think you're safe because there's a whole crowd of you kids now? I'll just come back with a

few of my deputies," Sheriff Routh declared. "And
the Pratcherds, too. Don't bother trying to hide."
The sheriff turned his horse around, kicking up dirt
and scattering the pile of kindling that the little kids
had been collecting. Suddenly, Jack wanted to yell
something—anything—at the man, but the words
wouldn't come. He stood there, furious and silent,
as the horse and rider dashed up the ravine and
rode off.

No one spoke for a moment after the sheriff left.

"Good riddance," Nicky said. "He can't threat-
en us."

Alexander took a deep breath. "No, he's seri-
ous. Did you see his face?" He turned to Jack and
Frances. "He'll be back."

Jack could only nod. He wasn't going to forget
that face anytime soon.

Frances's eyes were wild. "We can't just sit here
and wait for him to return!"

"So we'll fight back?" Lorenzo asked, picking
up a rock.

"No," said Alexander as he yanked down one
of the hammocks. "We have to get out of here, and
fast!" He tied the hammock into a bundle and began
to fill it with the bread that they'd taken from town.

After a moment, the others began to gather their things as well.

Frances crouched down to check the buttons on her little brother's shoes. Jack heard Harold ask, "Mrs. Routh isn't going to help us, is she? She was nice to us on the train."

Frances shook her head. "She has to obey the sheriff. He's her husband. We have to figure this out ourselves. . . ."

"No time to talk. Come *on!*" Alexander shouted.

Everyone began to move faster, except for Jack, whose feet had somehow turned heavy as he realized what was happening—what Alexander had just *decided.*

Just leave? he thought. *That was the solution?*

"Jack!" Quentin was standing in front of him now, looking anxious. "Hey, Jack, I . . ."

"In a minute," Jack said.

"But I have to tell you something . . ."

"It's all right, Quentin. No need to apologize." Jack knew it wasn't Quentin's fault that the sheriff had followed him to Wanderville, even if the other kids didn't believe him. There were more urgent things to deal with right now, like this crazy plan of Alexander's.

He stepped around Quentin and followed Alexander over to the old suitcase where they kept their provisions. "What do you mean, 'get out of here,' Alex?" Jack demanded. "Just ditch everything? What about the kids who are still at the Pratcherds'? Are we just going to run off and give up on them?"

Frances, who was nearby helping Harold with his coat, looked up, too. "Jack's right!" she said. "We can't just leave them."

Alexander turned and faced Jack. "It's too late for that. The sheriff found us. There's only one place we can go now."

"Where's that?" Frances asked.

"California," Alexander answered. Harold's eyes widened.

"There's a twelve o'clock train going west," Alexander continued, slinging a bundle over his shoulder. "We'll take the creek path and go into Whitmore. That will buy us some time because the sheriff will look for us here first."

Jack was shaking his head. "No! I still think we should stay and try to rescue the others at the ranch—"

"Jack," Alexander broke in. "We won't be any help to them if we all get caught!"

That was all Harold needed to hear. "I don't want the sheriff to catch us!" he cried.

"We're *not* going to get caught," Frances told her little brother. She looked up at Jack and Alexander. "We're going to do *something*, right?"

Alexander's eyes met Jack's. "That train's our only chance, and that's that."

That's that? Jack wanted to say more, but his mouth went dry. Alexander seemed to think he had all the answers. And he always had to have the last word.

Now we're here, Jack thought, keeping his eyes on the floor of the train car to avoid looking at Alexander. He couldn't believe they'd made it on board. But still he wished it all had gone differently—the rescue attempt, Quentin's escape, their sudden departure. And if Alexander had just bothered to listen to him . . .

Jack felt someone nudge his shoulder. Anka had crept over to where the boys were sitting. Anka, who had come all the way from Poland when she was younger—and now she was still traveling, still searching for a home. But somehow nothing seemed to get to her too much; she could always find a reason to laugh.

She smiled and took something out of her skirt pocket to show Jack and Alexander. It was the little painted wooden doll that she had brought out on her first night in Wanderville. Frances had made a small shelf in the crook of one of the trees, and it had been the perfect place for the doll to stand. It was one of the things that had made the wooded ravine feel like home.

"Remember the third law of Wanderville," Anka told them.

Jack understood. Back in the woods, he and Alexander and the rest of the children had created this last law—the law that meant that Wanderville could be anywhere they decided to build it. But Jack couldn't stop thinking about the Wanderville they'd just left.

Alexander grinned. "We're just on our way to the next place, that's all. Right, Jack?"

"Right," Jack said.

But he didn't mean it. Alexander *wasn't* right. They should have stayed in Kansas.

3
BRETHREN OF THE ROAD

"**D**o you think we're in California yet?" Frances's little brother whispered. "I want an orange."

"*Harold,*" Frances whispered back, "it'll be a long time before we get there."

Frances guessed that it had been about an hour since they left Whitmore. She was starting to get used to the jostled-all-over feeling that came from sitting on the floor of a moving freight car. The constant motion made the straw on the floor slowly travel across the boards, like a gently drifting current, and it was mesmerizing to watch. She began to think about California, too, and wondered whether she'd get to see the ocean. . . .

She was just starting to doze off to these thoughts when she felt the train slowing down.

"Why's the train stopping?" Harold asked.

Jack crept over to look out the side door, which had been left open a few inches. Alexander and Nicky were peering outside through wide chinks between the boxcar planks.

"I don't see a town or a station or anything," Nicky reported.

"Maybe it's a water stop," said Frances. "For the engine."

Just then, the hobo with the thousand-year-old voice sat bolt upright. "Kid sister is quite correct. And high time for some of my traveling brethren to join us here in the luxury coach."

Jack looked around the freight car and laughed. "Luxury coach?"

"Compared to riding the bumpers, 'tis," the hobo said. "You can call me Jim, by the by." Then he reached up and knocked against the side of the car. Three knocks, loud.

A moment later three knocks came from the outside. Then, suddenly, the side door slid open wider, and three dusty figures climbed in out of the sunlight.

Harold's face lit up. "Are you hoboes, too?" he asked them. He nudged George in excitement.

"Indeed we are," said one of the dusty men, who

licked the palm of his hand and used it to smooth back his hair. Frances could see he was the youngest of the three; he seemed to be about eighteen. He looked around and gave a big grin, followed by a sputtering cough.

"Riding the decks, eh?" said Jim. "Sounds as if you ate some dust."

"You were riding up *on top* of the train?" Frances couldn't believe it. The young hobo just nodded and grinned again.

"Time for introductions," declared Jim. He pointed to the sleeping man. "You've already met Dead John over here, and this here's Cooper and Fingy Jim." The two older hoboes shook hands with some of the boys.

"Wait, there are *two* Jims?" Frances asked.

"Show them what for you got your name, Fingy Jim," said the first Jim.

Fingy Jim held up his left hand. His fourth finger was a short stump and his fifth was missing. "Be carefulla them boxcar doors," he said.

Harold swallowed hard and shoved his hands deep in his pockets.

"What about you?" Frances asked the young hobo. "What's your name?"

He stretched out his legs as the train began to move again. "Well, I used to be known as The Oklahoma Baby. But it don't suit me any longer. Now I prefer to go by A-Number-One Nickel Ned Handsome," he said. "Or just Ned Handsome."

Frances didn't find Ned at all handsome on account of his sunburned face and missing front tooth, but he seemed kind enough.

"Those are good names," Harold said. "All of them." The other kids nodded.

"Thank you," said Ned Handsome. He looked around the car at the ten children. "So, are you folks ambulanters? A gypsy family?"

Alexander spoke up. "Not exactly. We're not gypsies, but we are on the move. Just like you, I guess."

"Not *'zactly*," said Ned. "*I'm* on the move. You're on the *run*. Escaping from somewheres or someones. It's plain to see."

Alexander and Jack exchanged nervous looks, and Quentin suddenly started to study his own shoes.

"But as you may have noticed by now," Ned continued, "us 'boes mind our own business."

Frances glanced around the car—the hobo named Jim appeared to have dozed off again,

Cooper and Fingy Jim were silently playing cards, and Dead John hadn't stirred. Meanwhile, the little kids, Harold and George, were hanging on Ned Handsome's every word.

"Besides, 'twasn't easy at my home when I was young," he said, his voice a little softer. "Sometimes better to hit the road."

"We all had a home in the woods. But we had to leave," Harold put in.

Ned cocked his head. "Is that so?"

Frances leaned in. "It's sort of a long story. . . ." But soon she and Jack and Alexander were taking turns telling Ned about the orphan trains, the sheriff, and the Pratcherds. Then they told him about Wanderville, and the swings they'd built, and the suitcase full of tinned food that they called the pantry.

"We built our own courthouse!" Harold said. "And we slept in the trees!"

The other kids joined in with their stories, and soon they were sharing their lunch with Ned—hunks of bread from Alexander's hammock and a couple of tins of sardines that Lorenzo had stashed in his pack. After a while Frances forgot about the rattling of the train and the way the wind whistled through the planks.

"Sounds like you had quite a paradise back there," said Ned Handsome. "How come you had to leave?"

Everyone fell silent for a moment. But then George piped up. "Because of Quentin," he said. "He gave away our hiding place."

"That's not fair!" Jack protested. "He was just trying to escape."

Quentin's face had gone beet red and his shoulders were hunched up nearly to his ears. Frances remembered how Quentin could be a bully sometimes, but she'd heard the Pratcherds had thrashed him extra hard, too. He seemed shaken up inside, like a bottle of fizzy cola.

"I *had* to run away from the ranch," he muttered. "I'll trounce anyone who says otherwise! And I've been trying t' tell you—"

Alexander broke in. "It's all right, Quentin. We believe you," he said. "Right, everyone?"

The other children nodded. Frances was fairly certain that Alexander *didn't* believe Quentin's story—she wasn't so sure she did herself—but the last thing anyone needed was for Quentin to get angry. Quentin settled down into a sullen silence, and nobody spoke for what seemed to Frances like an eternity. Even Fingy Jim and Cooper had paused their card game.

Ned Handsome cleared his throat. "Sounds like you could stand to borrow some of my luck," he declared. "If you run into more trouble and ever find yourself near Sherwood, Missouri, that is."

"What's in Sherwood?" Frances asked. She had never heard of the town.

Ned grinned. "Just a little something I stashed away."

Harold jumped up. "A treasure?"

"You could call it that. Something I found and set aside in case I ever needed it. But you folks might need it, too. If you want, I can tell you how to find it."

"Yes!" exclaimed Harold and George together.

"Er, all right," said Alexander, who sounded more skeptical.

"Very well, then," said Ned. "You begin at the depot in Sherwood, Missouri. . . ."

Frances reached into the side of her shoe and

drew out a pencil. Then she pulled out her *Third Eclectic Reader* and turned to the first bit of blank space she could find to write on.

Begin at depot in Sherwood, Missouri, she scribbled.

Ned went on, "And you'll have your boot on in the right direction. . . ."

"Don't you mean your *boots*?" Jack asked.

Ned shook his head. "You'll see what I mean if and when you get there. Anyways, then you'll cross an Indian, a saint, and one of our founding fathers."

Frances looked up from her writing. *"What?"*

"Write it just like I says, little sister. Then you give our founding father a right hook, and just keep going until you get mush. I know, it don't make sense now, but trust me, there will be mush! And then . . . look for a house with blue eyes that are always shut and has broken teeth. Go behind it into the woods. Then count steps. Every step has its own president. Once you get to Harrison, check the ground, and you should be on the right track."

"And?" Harold asked.

"And then you'll get to the right spot," Ned said. "I promise."

"Thanks," Jack said. "We'll be sure to . . . uh, remember it."

Frances looked down at what she'd written. It seemed like a puzzle. She had no idea where Sherwood, Missouri, was, but maybe there were clues she could figure out if she thought hard enough. Like, a *right hook*—was that his way of saying *turn right*?

She wanted to ask Ned Handsome, but by then he had started teaching the other kids a song— something about a place with mountains made of rock candy.

In the Big Rock Candy Mountains, all the cops
     have wooden legs,
And the bulldogs all have rubber teeth, and the
     hens lay soft-boiled eggs.
The farmers' trees are full of fruit, and the barns
     are full of hay.
Well, I'm bound to go where there ain't no snow,
Where the rain don't flow and the wind don't
     blow
In the Big Rock Candy Mountains.

"Ain't a real place," Ned said after he had sung it

to them. "But it's a song about how we wish things could be. And you can always make up new verses. In fact, I'll make up some just for you folks."

The next thing Frances knew, Jim was playing a harmonica in the corner, and they were all singing:

> *In the Big Rock Candy Mountains, all the sheriffs*
> *   are stone-blind,*
> *And the children from Wanderville don't pay 'em*
> *   any mind.*
> *The orphan trains don't go nowhere except to*
> *   Coney Island.*
> *Oh, the birds and the bees and the lib-er-ated*
> *   cheese.*
> *All the Pratcherds in jail, so we do as we please*
> *In the Big Rock Candy Mountains.*

They sang it five times over, enough to memorize it, until Jim put away his harmonica.

After that, Quentin and Lorenzo stayed in Ned's corner of the boxcar to hear him talk more about hobo life.

"Once I ran afoul of the cops in Cincinnati, and they clubbed me most diligently," Frances heard Ned tell them at one point.

"Wow!" said Lorenzo.

Meanwhile, Anka braided Sarah's hair, and Nicky and George played jacks in the corner.

"Can I play with them, too?" Harold asked Frances.

Frances hesitated. "Well . . ." Despite George's bookish glasses and the fact that he was a younger kid, the same age as Harold, George seemed like trouble sometimes. He'd swiped those jacks from right under the nose of the clerk at the Whitmore Mercantile last week, and Frances had been sure he'd get them all caught—over a set of lousy jacks.

But Harold had his *please please please* look on his face, so she shrugged and said, "Fine, go ahead."

Harold beamed and scurried over to George and Nicky's corner, leaving Frances, Jack, and Alexander by themselves.

The three said nothing for a while. They simply sat and swayed with the motion of the train.

"In the Big Rock Candy Mountains," Alexander sang softly, *"all the sheriffs are stone-blind."*

Jack just looked down into his lap. *"In the Big Rock Candy Mountains,"* he sang, *"nobody got left behind."*

Alexander sighed. "I know, Jack. I wish we

could have helped all the kids at the ranch escape. Believe me."

Frances felt a lump in her throat. "Me, too," she said.

Jack glanced up and smiled faintly at Frances. But, she noticed, he wouldn't even look at Alexander.

4
HOBOES DON'T PLAN

Jack hadn't known he'd dozed off until he felt someone shaking his shoulder. Hard. *Quentin*, Jack realized with a start. The big blond kid was shoving him now.

"I have to talk to you!" Quentin insisted. "I keep trying to tell you."

Jack rubbed his eyes and sat up. "Tell me what?"

"Not just *you*—all of you," Quentin said. "About why I had to run away from the Pratcherds by myself! But I'll explain to you first."

"You'd better explain to me, too," said Alexander, who had crept over to listen.

"Fine," Quentin said. "Look, I heard something at the Pratcherds' the other day. Mr. and Mrs. Pratcherd were walking by the barn when I had to muck the stalls. And they were talking, and I over-heard them. . . ."

"Saying what?" asked Frances, who had joined them, too.

"Saying . . . that they had to do something about all the runaways. 'Cause the suh, the suh-sighty . . . how do you say it? The *Society* didn't like that children were running away. 'Cause it doesn't look good."

"The Society for Children's Aid and Relief," Jack said, realizing. He remembered the office in New York that had sent them on the orphan trains to be "placed out."

"It could hurt the Society's reputation if a lot of kids escaped from the Pratcherds and said they were cruel."

"Right," said Quentin. "And then Mrs. Pratcherd said her sister who works for the Society was going to take care of it. Round up us kids and send us someplace else."

"A new placement, you mean?" Frances asked. "But maybe it would be a better place, right?"

Jack knew what she meant. They had all heard that sometimes that happened to orphan train kids—you'd be sent to another home if things didn't work out at the first one.

"No. That's just the thing," Quentin said, lowering his voice to almost a whisper. "That's why Mrs. Pratcherd's *sister* is coming out. She's that lady who was on our orphan train—the awful one. . . ."

"Miss DeHaven!" Jack shuddered. There'd been a rumor that the mean train chaperone was related to the ranch owner's wife, and now they knew it was true.

"That's her, all right. She's already on her way, coming out on another orphan train. But not just to take the farmhand kids away—she's also gonna get the sheriff to catch the rest of the ones who escaped."

Alexander looked stricken. "That's us."

Jack swallowed. "Did they talk about what Miss DeHaven would do with the kids they caught? Where she'd take them?"

"They didn't mention where 'zactly, but Mr. Pratcherd said . . ."

Quentin stopped for a moment. Jack looked around and saw that all the kids were listening now, along with Ned and two other hoboes who were awake. Quentin took a deep breath. "He said, '*Make sure they get worse than what they got here.*' And Mrs. Pratcherd said, 'Of course.'"

There was a terrible silence.

"What could be worse than the Pratcherds'?" Frances said. She put an arm around Harold.

"I don't know," Quentin murmured. "But then I got your note with the map, and I wanted to warn you. Because what if the sheriff caught you first? Then there wouldn't be anyplace the ranch kids could escape to. I didn't know what to do. . . ."

"So you just ran," Jack finished the thought for him. "I suppose I would have done the same thing."

"Not me," Alexander broke in. "I would've figured out a plan."

Quentin looked like he'd gotten a slap in the face.

"Well, like you said, Alexander"—Jack looked the older boy in the eye—"we can't change what happened." (Though truthfully, he still wished he could.) "We ought to talk instead about what we're going to do when we get to California."

Ned Handsome spoke up just then. "*California? How do you folks figure on getting there?*"

"On this train, of course," Alexander said. "Our plan started with getting out of Kansas on a west-bound train and . . ." Alexander's voice trailed off as he sat up straight and looked around the car.

Jack glanced around, too, and suddenly under-stood what the other boy was seeing: the sunlight that streamed between the wooden planks of the freight car's sides and roof. The light fell through the dusty air in slanted beams that were growing longer with the afternoon sun.

If they'd been heading west, Jack realized, they'd be traveling toward the afternoon sun. Not away.

"Cripes!" Jack blurted out. "We're going *east!*"

"Are we going back to New York?" Harold asked Frances, his eyes big.

"Not if we can help it," Frances told him.

She stomped across the car to where Jim was idly polishing his harmonica with a grimy handkerchief. "You heard my little brother say we were going to California when we first got on the train!" she said. "Why didn't you tell us this train was heading east?"

Jim just shrugged and kept polishing. "Figured you was planning t' get to California in a more inter-estin' fashion," he said.

Frances sighed and looked around. The other kids were all chattering in excitement and confusion. How could they have gotten on the wrong train? Anka pointed out they hadn't seen which direction the train came in from, since they'd all been hiding.

"We sure weren't thinking about which way it was

facing when we were making a run for it," Lorenzo recalled.

"It's not like we could've waited all day for the *right* train to come along," Sarah added.

"But I had a plan," Alexander said dejectedly.

"Hogwash. Hoboes don't plan."

Dead John had woken up, and he was glowering at them all from his corner of the car. "So stop talking your nonsense 'bout *plans* and such," he muttered. Then he turned and lay back down again, facing the wall.

"Er . . . what he means is that we 'boes just ride the rails and see where the day takes us," Ned Handsome explained.

"Are we hoboes now?" Harold asked.

Ned grinned. "Well, you ain't got a home and you're riding the rails, and you already said you ain't gypsy children, so the way I sees it, you're hoboes. Honorary hoboes, at least."

"But Ned," called out Fingy Jim, "they don't got their road names yet."

"Road names?" Frances asked.

"When you're traveling, you're not quite the same person as you are when you're not," Ned answered. "So you go by a road name. And you can't pick it—it's given to you on the road. But I can give 'em to you now, if you want. Who's first?"

"Me!" George waved his hand.

"Hmm . . ." Ned Handsome looked at him thoughtfully. "You've got spectacles, so we'll call you Glims, 'cause that's what some folks call 'em." George seemed to like that.

Next Ned turned to Nicky. "Skillet," he declared. "'Cause you're a little skinny and need to be reminded to eat breakfast."

"Sure thing," said Nicky.

Sarah shook her head. "I don't see the point of a road name," she protested, "if you're just going to give it up when you get settled somewhere."

Frances sighed. *That was just like Sarah to say that*, she thought, though she noticed Anka nodding a little, too.

"Fair 'nough, if that's how you feel," Ned replied. "How about the rest of you? If you want your road name, say 'aye.'"

Everyone else said *aye*, even Anka. Sarah shrugged and played with one of her braids.

Ned was able to think up names as soon as he looked hard at someone. Jack was Swindler Jack, and Lorenzo was dubbed Enzo the Tall. Alexander became Pennsylvania Kid, Anka was Petunia, and Harold was Little Tomato Can.

Frances wasn't sure she liked her road name. *"Gizzard?"*

"It's 'cause you got grit," said Ned.

Frances couldn't resist grinning then.

"Don't forget me!" Quentin cried. "Don't I get a road name?"

Ned looked at him. "You're Quentin, right? Hmm . . . seems like your name ought to have *tin* in it. How about Tin . . . *Whistle?* Because I bet with that crooked lip of yours, you can really whistle."

Quentin stood up and glared at Ned, his hands in fists. Frances thought he might actually slug the hobo. But Ned just smiled, and after a moment, Quentin seemed to relax and he sat back down.

"Tin Whistle, huh? I like that," he said. "Guess it doesn't matter if my face is kind of funny."

"That's right," Ned replied. "Because all kinds of funny stuff happens in life, and there's no sense in hiding our misfortunes. Being a hobo's 'bout learning to recognize that life takes you in certain directions for a reason. Even if you don't know the reason yet."

Frances wasn't quite buying all this. "So does that

mean life isn't going to take us to California?" she asked. "Since we're going the wrong way and all."

"It may *seem* like the wrong way, Gizzard my friend," Ned replied. "But if you hop off this train in Kansas City, you can get yourselves on a Santa Fe Express that goes more direct to California than the westbound trains on this line. And faster, too. If California is your destiny, life has a way of making it work. And in this case, it turns out going east a ways was the better way to go."

"You don't say," said Alexander. "How soon until we get to Kansas City?"

"Ain't more than an hour," Ned said.

Alexander turned to Frances and Jack. "This is our chance," he said. "Right?"

Jack nodded. "Let's go for it."

Frances wanted to agree, but she couldn't help but stare at the sunlight glowing through the slats of the boxcar. The sun was getting lower.

What if they were running out of chances?

5
WELCOME TO KANSAS CITY

According to Ned, the best way to slip off a train was to jump before it stopped. Otherwise the "bulls," the railroad men who patrolled the tracks, might catch you.

"Stay close to the rail yard fence," he advised. "And whatever you do, don't go inside the depot."

"But there's a place in there that has stick candy!" George said. He'd come out west on an orphan train that had stopped in Kansas City, and he'd seen the inside of the depot. More than once Jack had overheard him talking about it. "They got the cinnamon kind. Sassafras, wintergreen, horehound," George continued. "I swore that if I ever got away from the Pratcherds, I'd go back and get a whole lot of those sticks."

"Forget it, Glims," said Ned. "The town clowns are in the depot, too. The local cops, I mean. You'll want to stay clear of them and stick to the rail yard. That's where you'll look for the California train. . . ."

Jack did his best to pay attention to Ned, but all the while he kept his eyes on the space in the big sliding door, which provided a narrow window to the outside. The scenery was changing—they had just gone over a great iron bridge, over a river that glittered in the late-day sun. Now they were passing an area that was crisscrossed with wooden rail fences, and Jack could see that they were pens filled with cattle: dozens, no—*hundreds* of them crowded in this vast grid, bumping and nudging against one another. Jack realized it had to be the famous stockyards of Kansas City, where thousands of cattle and hogs and other livestock were sold. The strong, ripe smell of manure wafted in, and while he noticed some of the others in the train car were wrinkling their noses, he seemed to be the only one looking out at the view.

He'd never seen so many cows all at once. It was a stunning sight. Yet somehow it made him think about the orphan train and the ranch—all those times when he and all the other kids were made to line up and shuffle along single-file, herded together just like all that cattle. He turned away and tried to shake off the reminder.

A few minutes later, the wheels below them made a dull *thunk*, and the train began to slow down.

"It's almost time," Ned told them. Jack glanced outside again and saw taller buildings along the tracks; it was looking more like a city. Now they could all hear a growing din of clanging bells, chugging engines, and hoarse steam whistles.

The train was moving slowly enough that they could stand without losing their balance. Alexander shot up and helped to pull George and Harold to their feet. Not to be outdone, Jack stood, too.

The hoboes slid the freight car door open wider. Ned stuck his head out to look around, then turned back and nodded at the children. "You want to jump first?" he asked Jack.

"But I'm—" Alexander began. Jack could tell that Alexander wanted to go first, that he wanted to say that because he was the one who'd founded Wanderville—*he* was the leader. But he seemed to stop himself from saying so. Instead he went, "Go ahead, Jack. I'll make sure everyone gets off safely."

Jack nearly rolled his eyes at that. Still, he nodded

goodbye at the hoboes and shook Ned's hand, then stood ready at the doorway of the train car.

"Careful, now," Ned advised. "You'll stumble a bit when you hit the ground."

Jack grinned. "I know." It wasn't the first time he'd jumped off a train, after all. Or the last, he reckoned. The air rushed past his ears as he leaped— then, one heartbeat later, hit ground.

He steadied himself just in time to see Anka land a little way ahead of him. Next came George, hold- ing Sarah's hand, and Nicky, close behind them. Lorenzo did a daredevil leap, followed by Quentin. They'd all landed on a narrow stretch of gravel near the rail yard fence. Seven of them so far, all safe on solid ground. Which meant—Jack waited, holding his breath—three were still on board.

He watched the retreating train join the traffic in the bustling rail yard. "Alexander?" Jack called, not nearly loud enough. "Frances? Harold!"

Frances held her brother's hand so tight it had to hurt, but she wasn't letting him out of her sight around these tracks. They stood with Alexander and Ned in a tiny clearing at the center of the rail yard. Freight trains passed by on either side, and to

Frances it felt like being in a dark alley with sliding walls.

She was trying not to panic. "We're in the wrong place! We should have jumped when the others did."

" 'Twasn't safe," Ned reminded her.

Another train had blocked their way, and they'd had to leap off in the middle of the rail yard. Frances was glad that Ned was there—he'd left the other hoboes behind to help them—but the rail yard was so vast they couldn't see the other seven children.

Alexander looked as anxious as Frances felt. "How are we going to get back there? We can't be on these tracks, not with the railroad cops around."

But Ned Handsome just grinned. "We'll just head back a little the way we came!" And with that, he swung himself onto the rear platform of a nearby caboose as it crept by. "Come on!" he called.

It was easy enough to board the caboose, and soon they were slowly traveling in the opposite direction. *Wish we knew where to jump off again,* Frances thought. But the dusk shadows made it hard to see anything beyond the train cars. If they could just get to higher ground . . .

"Ned!" Frances said suddenly. "Can I ride up on top of the train? The way you do sometimes?"

"A girl like *you*?" Ned exclaimed. "You're not a-feared?"

"You said I had grit, didn't you?" Frances replied. She spotted a ladder from the rear platform to the roof of the caboose. "I'll just climb up that and see where our friends are."

Frances caught a glimpse of Alexander's surprised face as she grabbed the ladder rungs. She couldn't believe she'd just *decided* to climb on top of a train. The boys' breeches she wore made the climb easy.

"Wait, me, too!" Harold called from below. He could move like a little monkey, so of course *he* would want to clamber up as well. As soon as Frances reached the roof of the train car, she made room for her little brother to sit along the edge.

"We're in the sky!" Harold exclaimed.

Frances agreed. Sitting up so high was like being on a fire escape back in New York. Well, a *moving* fire escape. The sky was still bright, and she could feel a warm, gritty breeze on her arms. Best of all, she could see the end of the rail yard, where Jack and Sarah and the others had gathered.

"I see them!" she called down to Alexander on

the caboose platform. "All we need to do is ride this down to where they are!" She saw fewer sets of tracks over there, and it would be easier to navigate the slowly passing trains.

Alexander grinned. "Good job!" he called back.

"The coast is clear of the railroad bulls, for now't least," Ned said once Frances and Harold had climbed back down to the platform. "And just like before, jump when I tells you, and look both ways."

"We're sure glad for your help," Alexander told Ned.

"And I got to ride on top of a train!" Harold exclaimed. "I can't believe we did that!"

Frances felt herself smile. She couldn't believe it, either.

"Ain't nothing," Ned replied. "Good luck to you and all the other Wanderville citizens," he said. He looked over at Frances. "Too bad you won't be down near Sherwood to see what I left there. But if you get to California, you won't need it anyways."

Frances felt an odd little shiver at the mention of the treasure. She was glad she'd written down the hobo's instructions. *Who knows?* she thought. *Maybe someday . . .*

Ned interrupted her reverie. "In about five seconds, there's your spot to jump!" he said, pointing to a stretch of gravel by the rail yard fence.

Since it took Frances about five seconds to say, "Thank you, A-Number-One Nickel Ned Handsome!" her jump was perfectly timed, and she hardly stumbled when she hit the ground. A moment later, Alexander, with Harold riding piggyback, leaped and landed safely, much to her relief.

The spot where Frances stood wasn't far from where the other kids had jumped from the first train, and now they were all running over to see her and the boys. Jack was the first to reach her, and he shook his head in amazement—or perhaps, Frances suspected, relief.

"Well, if it isn't Gizzard, the Pennsylvania Kid, and Little Tomato Can!" he said, smiling wide. "Glad you decided to join us after all."

Now all they had to do was find the right train. But navigating the Kansas City rail yard turned out to be harder than Frances had thought it would be.

"What's the name of the train Ned told us to catch again?" she asked.

"It's the . . ." Jack shut his eyes as if to better

remember. "It's the Atchison, Topeka, and Santa Fe," he answered. "Uh . . . right?" He didn't seem too sure.

"Wait," said Alexander. "Is that all *one* train? Or three different trains?"

"Of course it's one train!" Jack looked at Frances. "Isn't it?"

Frances gazed out over the many crisscrossing sets of tracks at the dark, hulking train cars that slid by. She strained her eyes to read the letters painted on the sides, willing the right name to appear. But she could only make out a few words here and there—*Chicago, Alton.* Were those the names of the trains or of their destinations? Meanwhile, the sky still held the last of the daylight, but everything else seemed to be rapidly fading into dusk.

Sarah spoke up, her voice wary. "It's getting dark. What should we do?"

"Maybe we should wait until morning to hop a train," Jack suggested.

"And risk getting caught here?" Alexander said. "Where will we go for the night?"

Frances peered out at the city block beyond the rail yard fence. There were lamps glowing in some of the businesses, though the windows were grimy and the lights hardly looked welcoming; one of the places appeared to be a saloon.

"We shouldn't go too far," she said to Alexander. "But Jack's right. We should wait till morning, when we can know if we're on the right train. Let's find someplace nearby to sleep." Frances noticed just then that Harold was rubbing his eyes, and George looked tired, too. It had been a long day, she realized, and she suddenly felt foggy with exhaustion. Had it been just that morning that they'd been in Wanderville?

Anka and Nicky spotted a little toolshed in an alley just beyond the fence.

There was no door, but the floor was dry and, if some of the kids sat upright and leaned against the walls, there was just enough space for all of them to sleep. Which is what Frances did, with Harold curled up against her.

"Frannie?" Harold whispered, looking up at the cobwebbed ceiling of the shed. "Can we find a better house tomorrow for all of us?"

Frances sighed and stroked his hair. "We'll be back on a train tomorrow. This is just for tonight."

"But *after* the train, we'll be in California, right?

Where we can stay?" His voice became scratchier. "It doesn't even have to be California, as long as . . ."

"Harold," Frances said in her *hush-up* tone, "wherever we go, I'll be here. With you."

"Okay." And in another few moments he was asleep.

Still feeling the motion of the train in her limbs and wondering again about the treasure at the end of Ned's instructions, Frances soon drifted off, too. She dreamed about houses with eyes and founding fathers who turned to mush.

When Jack's voice woke her up, she could see morning light through the doorway of the shed. She looked around at the others sleeping. Somehow the floor of the shed seemed less crowded than it had been last night. Were all the boys sleeping outside?

But Jack was already up and standing. And shouting.

"Wake up!" he cried. "There's only seven of us here. Who's missing?"

6

INSIDE THE DEPOT

Three boys were gone: Quentin, Lorenzo, and George. And there was a note, from Quentin.

Jack had found it held down by a rock in the corner of the shed that Quentin had claimed the night before. The paper was thick and appeared to have been torn out of a book. Frances brought over her old *Third Eclectic Reader* and showed him where Quentin must have torn the flyleaf out. "Guess he borrowed my pencil, too," she said.

Jack was reading the words over and over again, written in a wobbly script:

Dear Jack & ever one,
    Enzo & me are gone to hop a train
somewhere. Ned told us lots about the hobo

life & it sounds real good. He say hoboes work
sometimes picking fruit but you can leave
anytime you dont like it. Want some pocket
money & nobody telling us whats what. Be sides
I feel real bad about all you haveing to leave
Wandervill cause of me & maybe better if I go.

Enzo say bye & thanks too.
Tin Whistle & Enzo

Sarah grabbed the note. "But where's George?"
she said. "He's gone as well! The note doesn't mention him."

By now Anka and Nicky and Harold were awake
and had gathered around, and Alexander was pacing
back and forth by the rail yard fence.

"Did anyone hear them leave? Anyone see anything?" he asked.

Jack felt sunk. All he'd wanted to do was bring
the kids at the Pratcherd ranch to Wanderville,
but when that had failed, he was glad that at least
Quentin had joined them. Wasn't it better to stay
together?

Just then Harold spoke up. "I know something,"
he said in a small voice. "I-I didn't see Quentin and

Lorenzo. They were gone when I woke up. But . . . I know where George is. . . ."

"*Where*, Harold?" Frances snapped.

Harold looked over in the direction of the depot building, which loomed in the near distance like a castle with its tower and pointed gables and turrets. "He said he was going to get some candy," he mumbled. "Like the kind he had when his train stopped here before."

"Oh, no," Jack said. "He'll be caught for sure if he tries to steal here in Kansas City." His stomach lurched as another thought came to him, too: What if Sheriff Routh had sent out word that they were runaways?

Alexander seemed to be thinking the same thing. "Let's hope that they aren't already looking for kids on the loose." Turning to Jack, he added, "You and me had better go find him."

"We're *all* going," Frances declared. "Remember what Ned said about the town cops in the depot. What if they caught you, too? Then we'd never know what happened."

"Good idea," Jack said.

Alexander, meanwhile, obviously didn't agree, judging from the way he quickened his pace to walk ahead of the other six kids as they made their way to the depot.

Jack rushed to catch up with him. "Look, Alex, it's better if we stick together," he said upon reaching him. "That way, when we find the train to California, we can all get on it at the same time."

Alexander's jaw was set and his face was steely. "We should've hopped a train last night instead of staying here," he muttered. "Blast that Quentin. Lorenzo, too."

"You didn't have to be so mean to Quentin, you know."

"Oh, so it's *my* fault that he left? Just like it's *my* fault that we got on the wrong train?"

"I never said that!" Jack protested.

"Both of you, pipe down!" said Frances in the mother-hen tone she usually used with Harold. "We're getting close to the depot."

Kansas City's Union Depot was no Grand Central, Jack thought, but it was still plenty big, with long corridors and high-ceilinged waiting rooms. Porters pushing dollies loaded with baggage seemed to come from all directions, and people streamed through every doorway. There were even stray dogs in the depot—Jack noticed more than one mutt roaming around the waiting areas and nosing through the sandwich wrappers and other litter beneath the benches.

"Look! Water!" Anka cried as she rushed over to a drinking fountain across one of the hallways. The other kids followed, and Jack could no longer ignore his own thirst. Anka grabbed one of the tin cups that hung from the spout on a chain and filled it again and again for everyone with the good, clean cold water. Even though it was a risk coming into the depot, Jack thought, at least they'd gotten a much-needed drink.

He peered into the bustling lobby, looking for the candy stand, hoping George hadn't gotten to it yet. He spotted a newsstand, a peanut cart, a man handing out leaflets, and . . .

"Apples," Frances whispered. "Do you suppose they're free? There's no price on the signs."

Behind the man with the leaflets were two plainly dressed young women with bushel baskets of apples at their feet. They were softly singing hymns, and one of the baskets bore a placard that said AN APPLE A DAY FOR HEALTH & TEMPERANCE. Next to them were an older woman and a teenage boy holding signs that said PRAY WITH US and STOP THE SALOONS.

"Nothing's free if it comes with a sermon," Jack muttered.

"It's only a sermon about how whiskey is bad," Frances said. "Which it *is*. I'd say that's worth an apple or two. What've you got against folks like those?"

"Nothing, I just—"

"Hey!" Nicky broke in. "There's George!"

The boy was racing through the lobby in a zigzag fashion, his worn shoes sliding along the tile with each turn. He zipped right past Jack and the others and darted into a waiting room.

Jack looked back into the lobby in time to see the stationmaster in pursuit.

"Somebody stop that little hooligan!" the man was bellowing. "Check his pockets!" The stationmaster had lost sight of George, but there was only one corridor in this direction, so it was only a matter of time before he figured out where the boy had gone.

Alexander caught Jack's eye. He was nodding at something—the drinking fountain's faucet.

Jack understood. He stepped over to the faucet and casually placed the tin cup over the drain. Then he cranked open the tap. Water started to fill the little basin beneath the spout.

Anka's eyes grew wide when she realized what was happening, and the other kids backed away from the basin as it began to overflow.

"Walk fast, but don't run," Alexander told everyone in a low voice. "Follow me." He headed in the direction George had scurried.

Jack couldn't resist looking back to see what had happened. There was a puddle spreading into the lobby, and the stationmaster was shouting at one of the porters. Another porter was using a broom to try to shoo away the stray dogs that had come to lap up the water.

"I think they forgot about George." Alexander laughed. "*Now*, let's run!"

"I see him!" Sarah whispered to Frances. They were checking the waiting rooms one by one for George. They'd split up to save time—Jack and Harold were searching with them, and the other three had gone to look along the other side of the hall.

"Where is he?" Frances asked.

"Hiding behind those trunks." There were half a dozen wooden trunks lined up near the door. Sarah ran over to them and yanked George out by the arm.

"Yowch!" he yelled.

"Children!" said a scolding voice behind them.

Frances turned and saw a short but substantial woman heading their way. "Let me see your tickets," she said. As the woman brushed off her uniform coat, Frances noticed a brass pin on her lapel. DEPOT MATRON, it read.

"We, uh . . . we don't have tickets," Frances blurted out. "Because . . . we're waiting to meet our papa's train."

The depot matron looked them over: Jack, Sarah, Frances, Harold, George. *"All* of you?" she said. "The same papa?"

"We're going to help carry his bags," Harold volunteered.

" 'Cause he got a wooden leg," George added.

Jack suddenly broke into a very odd coughing fit.

"We'll sit here *quietly,*" Sarah said quickly, grabbing George by his jacket collar and pulling him over to a bench. Frances did the same with Harold, and Jack plunked down, too.

"Very well," the depot matron said. "Don't let me hear you again."

Frances held her breath until the matron turned away. "We'll just wait here until she leaves," she whispered to Jack and Sarah.

Jack peeked over his shoulder. "But she's sitting on the bench behind us."

"Then we'll just have to linger," Frances said with a sigh. She shifted in her seat on the bench and tried to distract herself by practicing her best posture.

A few minutes passed and the depot matron still did not move. In fact, she had struck up a very spirited conversation with one of the waiting passengers.

"Miss Lily!" the matron said. "Always a pleasure to chat whenever you pass through Kansas City! So, which way are you headed?" she asked her friend. "Going back to New York?"

"No," her companion replied. "Whitmore, Kansas. One of my *favorite* places . . ."

Frances's throat went tight. She'd heard that voice before.

The voice continued. "My *dear* sister and her husband are in *utmost* need of my help. And *of course* you're aware of my *charity work* with the *Society*. . . ."

Next to Frances, Harold stiffened, and when she

looked over at Jack and Sarah, their faces were ashen. They knew the voice, too: melodic and refined—but with an unmistakable edge. Frances didn't dare turn around, but she could picture the stylish traveling dress, the pinched smile, the fancy ribboned badge . . .

"So you're about to go on chaperone duty, then?" the depot matron asked.

"Yes," said Miss DeHaven. "The train's due in half an hour. Another orphan train."

7
A MOST ANXIOUS EAVESDROPPING

Don't move, Frances thought. She was too nervous to even mouth the words to Harold, much less whisper them, so she hoped he could somehow hear her thoughts as he sat next to her. *Quiet as a mouse.* They were all quiet now, she and Harold and George, Jack and Sarah—not just to escape the depot matron's attention, but to listen to what Miss DeHaven was saying.

". . . the youngest ones are less *troublesome*, to be sure. Of course, one must give their grimy little faces a good *scrubbing* before they come off the train so that they're rosy-cheeked and *presentable*, and if they cry a few tears, it's no matter."

Frances could feel her face growing hot as she listened.

"Besides," Miss DeHaven continued, "I daresay it's the weepy orphans who get picked first, especially by *sentimental* people who want these waifs to be *family*." The more she talked, the less musical her voice sounded.

". . . yes, and as for the older ones, they're just dreadful. Guttersnipes. Ungrateful for the chance to breathe country air and learn the value of hard work. My sister and her husband have taken in several of them, but they're wholly out of control—running away, spreading lies all over town, tormenting my poor nephew . . ."

Out of the corner of her eye, Frances could see Jack smirk a little, and she remembered his story about how the kids at the ranch had thrown potatoes at Rutherford Pratcherd after he punished them with beatings and cracked his whip at them.

"Terrible," the depot matron was saying. "What can be done about them?"

"Place them elsewhere," Miss DeHaven replied. "And I'm heading back to Whitmore to do exactly that. . . ."

So what Quentin had overheard was true, Frances realized. Miss DeHaven and the Pratcherds were going to take all the ranch children someplace else. There had been too many escapes, too many "troublemakers." They could be replaced—maybe even by the children who were coming on the orphan train Miss DeHaven was waiting for right now.

Next to Frances, Sarah was nervously smoothing her braids. No doubt she—and Jack—were wondering the same thing Frances was, the one question that Quentin never quite answered: *Where will the ranch children be taken?*

The women were speaking in lower voices now, and Frances and the others had to strain to hear them.

". . . down to St. Louis, where they will be enrolled in Mr. Edwin Adolphius's school, and—"

"Edwin *Adolphius*?" the matron interrupted. "But doesn't he own a canning factory?"

Miss DeHaven paused and cleared her throat. "Mr. Adolphius runs an excellent *industrial school* for indigent youth. *Perhaps* there is also a factory."

Frances couldn't believe it. She was itching to write down everything she'd just heard and wondered if she could pull out her book and pencil without looking suspicious.

But just then came the scuffle of running feet, the noise quickly getting closer. She looked up, and so did Jack.

"There you are!" Alexander called out when he saw them. He ran toward the bench, followed by Anka and Nicky. "You found George! We ought to get out of here like the blazes!"

"That stationmaster sure don't like the look of us!" Nicky added.

Frances stood up, her chest pounding in panic. She saw Jack try to put his finger to his lips, but it was no use. The boys' voices could be heard throughout the whole waiting room.

The depot matron stood, too. "You said you were waiting for your papa," she said, her voice rising with suspicion.

"Whose pa?" Nicky asked.

The matron gasped. "You little liars!"

Miss DeHaven had turned and was staring intently at them. Frances felt an urge to hide her face, but she knew it would make things worse.

"You children . . . where did you *come* from?" Miss DeHaven asked.

Nobody said a word. Alexander and Anka backed away a few steps. *Should we try to escape?* Frances wondered. Nobody seemed to know what to do.

"Has no one taught you to speak when spoken to?" Miss DeHaven hissed. Then her gaze fell on

Nicky. "Boy," she said, "you speak with an accent. New York—the slums."

Nicky was too stunned to answer.

But Frances glared back at Miss DeHaven. "We . . . we don't know what you're talking about," she said, grabbing Harold's hand. "We were all just leaving." Her heart was thumping hard and her legs were trembling. From somewhere outside a train whistle shrieked and it felt like a scream from deep in her brain.

Suddenly, Harold yanked his hand out of Frances's, his eyes wide. *"I think that's Papa's train!"* he yelled. *"We'd better run for it! Run!"* And just like that, Frances's little brother was off like a shot, hurtling straight out of the waiting room.

She and the other six children trailed right behind.

8
THE NOT-ORPHANS

"That was close," Jack whispered when he could finally catch his breath enough to speak.

The children had made it all the way outside the depot and had dashed around to the side of the building, out of sight from the front doors. They'd stopped for the sake of Nicky, who occasionally wheezed when he ran.

Alexander grinned. "That was some quick thinking, Harold," he said, reaching down and ruffling the seven-year-old's red hair.

But Jack wasn't smiling. "You should know when to keep your voice down," he told Alexander.

"How was I supposed to know that Miss DeHaven was there?" Alexander protested. "And besides, what could she do to us—rap our knuckles?"

"She can do plenty more than that," Jack said. "You should have been there when she was talking to the depot matron. . . ." He and Frances and Sarah quickly explained to the others what they'd just overheard.

"She's awful," Frances said with a shudder.

Anka nodded. "Her face has hate."

"Do you think she recognized us?" Sarah asked. "Does she know we're the kids who escaped from the Pratcherds?"

"I don't know," said Jack. "She was definitely suspicious. And she knows we're from New York."

On one hand, Jack figured Miss DeHaven despised most kids, especially the down-and-out ones, and couldn't be bothered to remember every orphan train rider. On the other, there'd been a moment back in the waiting room when she'd looked him in the eye, and he was sure she knew who he was. Either way, it was better to stay out of her sight.

By now Nicky's wheezing had settled down.

"Let's head out now," Alexander said. He turned and took a couple of steps in the direction of the rail yard, then stopped short. The stationmaster was right in front of him.

Jack spun around and saw three porters blocking the other direction.

"There you are," the stationmaster said with a sneer. "We're here to escort you little wretches to your train."

"What are you talking about? *We're* going to California!" Alexander sputtered as they were being marched back into the depot. The stationmaster had a steel grip on Alexander's arm and Jack's, too, and the rest of the kids were being firmly led along by the porters.

"I know orphan trash when I see it," said the stationmaster, "and I will not have you gangs of street urchins in my depot picking pockets and begging."

"But we're not—" Frances tried to protest, but the stationmaster went right on talking.

"And it just so happens there is a lady here *right now* whose job it is to take care of cases like you. Get you kids out of here, send you someplace where you'll be useful and not such a blasted nuisance. There's a train about to come in. . . ."

They were in the depot lobby now, and Jack couldn't even hear his own stumbling footsteps over

the din—hundreds of tapping feet that in the echo-
ing hallway formed the rhythm of a grim march.
Marching him to his doom, he thought.

The stationmaster continued, "It's a train full of
other orphans like you. The lady here says she can fit
you on. Might even get a sandwich. Then you'll be
someone else's problem. . . ."

The crowd surrounding Jack seemed to blur as
he recognized the figure down at the head of the
corridor—the way she stood perfectly still in her
fashionable dress with the puffed sleeves. The lobby
tiles were highly polished, and Miss DeHaven stood
in her own dark reflection.

Jack looked around frantically. Was there another
door to the outside? Anything?

"Jack!" Alexander whispered next to him. "We'll
make a run for it. Come on!"

"Run for *what*?" Jack hissed. "There's nowhere
to go!"

Alexander glared at him, but Jack just shook his
head. The lobby was too vast, and all the other corridors were too far away for all of them to attempt
an escape.

Still, Jack's mind kept racing as he searched for

a way out. They were about to walk past the holy folks, the ones with the signs who were handing out leaflets and apples. Jack noticed the man and the older woman—his wife, Jack supposed—standing with their hands clasped, softly singing a hymn. PRAY WITH US, the sign read. Jack stared hard at it. *Pray*, he thought. *Pray for a way to get out of this mess. . . .*

Then he wrenched his arm free from the station-master's grip. *"No!"* he yelled.

"What did you say, boy?" the stationmaster growled.

"No, we're not orphans!" He pointed to the pray-ing couple. "We're with them!"

The man and woman ceased with their hymns and looked up, blinking. Behind them, the young women and the teenage boy stared with wide eyes.

"Y-yes," Frances began. "We *told* the station matron our papa was here!" She pulled her arm free, too. "That's our family right there."

The porters exchanged confused looks. One of them let go of Harold and George, who rushed over to Frances and Jack, nodding in agreement.

"Liars!" spat the stationmaster. "You're lying lit-tle wretches!" He shot a look over to Miss DeHaven, who was marching toward them now, her face set in a strange, tight smile. "Now, here's the lady; you're going with *her*—do you understand?"

"No!" Jack yelled, but the stationmaster grabbed his arm even harder. At the same time, the porters seized Frances and the two youngest boys again. "I told you . . . ," Jack protested.

"That's enough. Let's go," said the stationmaster.

"No, *that's* enough," said a deep voice. It was the praying man. "Lay your hands off God's children!"

9
THE FAMILY THAT PRAYS TOGETHER

To Frances it seemed as if everything stood still after the praying man spoke.

Jack stood with his mouth half open. The stationmaster's eyes bulged in surprise, and Miss DeHaven paused midstride. But Frances could still feel her own breathing, could hear herself exhaling slowly.

And then the man said, "The boy is telling the truth."

"Indeed he is," the woman next to him added.

Suddenly, Frances's arm was free. The porter had let her go. She looked around to see that the other kids were no longer being restrained, but they were looking to her and Jack to see what they should do. So Frances took a few tentative steps toward the couple. Jack and Alexander did the same.

The stationmaster straightened up. "Just what's going on here, Reverend Carey?" he asked the man.

"I might ask you the same thing," said the Reverend.

The woman—Mrs. Carey, Frances guessed—picked up one of the apple bushels and held it so that Harold and George could choose apples. Which they did, gladly.

"Er, we've had a problem here in the depot with waifs and runaways," the stationmaster said. "And we have our ways of dealing with them."

"And you thought these children needed to be . . . dealt with?" the Reverend replied.

"Excuse me, Reverend," said the stationmaster. "We didn't realize they were with you. Er . . . they *are* with you, is that right?"

Reverend Carey looked over to his wife just then, who nodded back. "I assure you," he said. "These children are not alone in the world."

Frances thought it was interesting how he answered the question without *really* answering it. She never knew a preacher to be clever—the ones who ran the orphanage back in New York gave dull, glum sermons on Sundays. But Reverend Carey seemed sharp.

"Though they are certainly spirited," Mrs. Carey said, looking kindly down at George.

The young women behind them smiled gently. Frances wondered if they were the Careys' daughters. They had the same thick, chestnut hair as the Reverend, and both had chins like Mrs. Carey. The teenage boy, who looked to be about eighteen, resembled Mrs. Carey, too. Like her, he had stick-straight hair the color of clay.

Miss DeHaven approached. "Mr. Barron," she said to the stationmaster. "*Kindly* explain what is *happening*."

Mr. Barron looked baffled. "You said these children were orphans, but . . . the Reverend here . . ."

One of the porters spoke up. "Ma'am, Preacher Carey and his wife have been coming to the depot for years. Once a month or so they come from downstate Missouri to spread the good word and speak out against salooning."

It was just as Frances had thought—the Careys preached about the evils of liquor. Well, from what she'd seen of the drunks on the Bowery, there was good reason to do so.

The porter continued, "They're decent folks,

the Careys. They've got a whole passel of children, I believe, all different ages."

The other porters nodded at this. The stationmaster shrugged, and Miss DeHaven narrowed her eyes.

"Very well," she said, her eyes darting up at the lobby clock. "Mr. Barron, the train I'm meeting arrives very shortly. *Some* of the orphans on that train will find immediate placements here in Kansas City. . . ."

At the mention of *placements*, Frances's stomach lurched. She knew that those kids would be lined up, and strangers would come and choose them—even separate them from their siblings—and they'd go off to unknown fates.

Miss DeHaven continued, "And then the remaining children and I will board another train at twelve thirty-five and continue west. *So*, Mr. Barron, if you discover *any* orphans here in the depot before then"—she shot a look straight at Frances—"then there will certainly be room for them to join us."

And with that, she turned and strode away down the corridor, glancing once more at the clock.

The stationmaster tipped his hat in the direction Miss DeHaven had gone. "I'll be sure to check," he called. "Sometimes we mistake people's children for beggar orphans. And sometimes . . . it's the other way around."

He said that last part loud enough for all the kids to hear. Then he walked off across the lobby. The porters, shrugging, followed him.

Frances felt almost limp with relief.

"Thank you, mister," Jack said. "I mean . . . Reverend." He approached the minister to shake his hand.

After a moment, Alexander stepped up, too. But instead of shaking his hand, he hung back. "Reverend?" he asked. "Why did you suddenly just . . . *help* us?"

"I noticed you all when you first came in here," the Reverend replied. He motioned dramatically toward the water fountain. "You helped each other when you were thirsty, and I could see that you were good children who deserved mercy."

"It was as simple as that?" Frances asked.

"Sometimes it is, child," said Mrs. Carey. She nodded gently at Frances, then turned to exchange a beaming smile with her husband.

Frances felt a twinge of doubt. The Careys seemed like the sort of folks who did nice things but who were awfully proud of doing them. It didn't necessarily make them nice themselves.

Just then Harold nudged her to hand her an apple. "These are the best!" he said, biting into his. Anka and George were helping themselves as well. Nicky and Sarah stood off a little way, still hesitant. The Careys' son and daughters stared back, their faces blank. As for the Reverend and Mrs. Carey, they were now putting their heads together in discussion.

Frances looked over at Jack. She could tell he had the same thought she had: *What next?*

Then she heard Mrs. Carey ask her husband, "Do we have enough for eight more train fares?"

The Reverend nodded and smiled at Frances and her friends.

"Eight children," he said. "A blessed number! In the Bible, eight is the number signifying abundance. We're very fortunate today."

Frances couldn't imagine how she and the other kids were anyone's good luck, but the Careys seemed to think so.

Mrs. Carey turned to Alexander. "Have you all got your things? If so, we'll get right on the eleven twenty-five to Bremerton."

Alexander stood there, looking a little stunned. "Er . . . what's in Bremerton?" he asked finally.

The Reverend clapped his hand on Alexander's shoulder. "Why, *home*, of course!"

Frances glanced down at Harold and saw his mouth drop open at the word *home*. She squeezed his hand anxiously.

"Dear," Mrs. Carey said to her husband with a chuckle, "we really ought to learn their names first."

10
QUESTIONS, AND A CLUE

All the names were learned soon enough.

The Careys' daughters were Olive and Eleanor. The son was Jeb. They were aged seventeen, sixteen, and fifteen, with Jeb being the youngest. Jack couldn't tell which of the girls was older, or even who was Olive and who was Eleanor, because they looked nearly alike and they hardly spoke during the walk to the train platform.

It felt extremely strange to Jack that he and the other kids were now following this family through the depot. But it sure seemed like their only choice at the moment. The stationmaster had made it clear that they'd be put on an orphan train if they stayed in the depot. And the way he saw it, getting on a train with the Carey family wasn't much different from hopping on a freight car—either way, you didn't know what to expect.

Alexander walked next to him, his hands in his pockets, his face hard to read. Was he mad at what Jack had done back in the depot? Jack knew Alexander had been trying to figure out how to get away from the stationmaster. He'd had a better idea, that was all. Now they needed a plan for when they arrived at the Careys'. They'd have to escape from that place, too, but Jack hoped it would be easier.

When they reached the platform, he looked over at the others. Frances held her little brother's hand and studied the clock on its big iron stand—the time was eleven fifteen. Anka and Sarah were whispering among themselves. George and Nicky were being fussed over by Mrs. Carey. Jack thought about the last time all of them stood waiting on a train plat-form—it was back in New York, just before they boarded the orphan train at Grand Central. He felt a familiar old pang as he remembered saying good-bye to his mother and father; he'd had no idea what would happen next. What lay ahead for him and the other kids now, Jack realized, was no less uncertain than it had been back then.

But this time he would at least ask questions. He turned to the Reverend. "Sir, I was wondering—"

"Yes," said Reverend Carey. "You must all be wondering what Mrs. Carey and I mean by bringing you back with us."

Everyone nodded, and he continued. "We have a farm near Bremerton. We can always use help with the chores and in the apple orchards. There's plenty of room for you to stay, both around the farm and even in the house."

Mrs. Carey went on to explain that they had six children—three were grown now, and Olive, Eleanor, and Jeb were the youngest.

"So we are accustomed to having children around," the Reverend said.

"Will we be—" Frances's little brother started to ask.

"Not now," Frances broke in. "The train's coming in." It was pulling into the station, and they would be boarding in a moment.

Harold went quiet, and Jack felt a beat of dread as he realized what the boy's full question to the Reverend would have been.

Will we be your *children?*

Once they were on the train, Jack slid into a seat next to Alexander, who had chosen a spot in the coach that was as far back from the Careys as possible.

"So what now?" Jack asked, his voice low. "We ought to escape as soon as the Careys reach their stop, right?"

"I say we stay long enough for the Careys to make us a decent dinner. Then we'll take our leave in the morning," Alexander said, like the matter was settled.

"Are you sure that's a good idea? The more we depend on these folks, the harder it'll be to leave," said Jack. "At least for some of us." He'd noticed the way Anka's and Sarah's faces had brightened a little when the Reverend mentioned living in their house. Harold's, too.

Alexander shrugged. "The Careys mean well and all, but they're Holy Rollers, and their life isn't the life for us. Everyone can see that."

Jack wasn't so sure. "Well, Quentin and Lorenzo sure thought that hoboing was the life for *them*."

"There you go again, blaming me for being mean to Quentin," Alexander hissed. "And for everything else, too."

It seemed to Jack that they kept arguing about

the same blasted thing. "I never said that. I just want us all to stay together."

"Me, too," Alexander muttered. "It's just hard work keeping everyone together, that's all." He turned away to lean against the windowsill and watch the scenery speed by. He didn't say anything more after that.

Jack found another empty seat across the aisle, where in the very next row Jeb Carey and either Olive or Eleanor were sitting quietly. Jeb looked up from reading a small brown book called *The Noble Work of Missionaries* and gave him a faint smile. "Pa's sermons are kind of long, but he's all right," he said.

Jack nodded.

"You'll all get sick of apples, too," Jeb added. Then he went back to his book.

With no one to talk to, Jack rested his head back against the seat. He closed his eyes and listened to the rhythm of the train. The noise drifted further and further back in his head as he began to nod off.

"Jack!" Frances was nudging him. "Jack!"

He shook himself awake. The train was quiet. "Are we there?" He began to stand up.

"Not yet!" Frances whispered. "But look!" She was in the aisle, pointing out the window.

Jack turned to see a train platform outside—just a quiet depot in a small town, nothing unusual. "Look at what?" he asked Frances.

"The *sign*!" Frances said excitedly. "The name of the *town*!"

Jack saw it on the platform: SHERWOOD. He'd just heard that town name . . . where?

"It's where Ned Handsome left his secret stuff!" Frances exclaimed. "Whatever it is, he said we could find it if we were ever in Sherwood." The train began to slowly move again as Frances continued. "We're just passing through Sherwood right now, but it's the last stop before Bremerton! I asked the conductor about it. The place where we're going is just the next town over, and I wrote down all of Ned's clues, and just now I was looking out the window and . . . and *look*! Quick! That store across the street!"

She yanked Jack up by his jacket collar so that he could get a better view. He scanned the storefronts of Sherwood, Missouri, as they slid by the window. They were all dull, except for a cobbler shop on the corner that had a big wooden boot hanging over its door instead of a sign.

"The *boot*," Frances said proudly. "It's one of the clues."

Jack tried to get a second look, but the train was moving too fast, and the town was already behind them. Truthfully, he couldn't believe that Frances was taking this business about buried hobo treasure so seriously. Then again, so much had happened to them in the past two days that anyone would be a little crazy. And tired and hungry . . .

Jack found himself so ravenous all of a sudden that he reached into his pocket and pulled out the apple the Careys had given him. It was red on one side and golden on the other. Jack bit right into the red side. It was tart and his mouth puckered, but that was what made an apple good as far as he was concerned.

The crunching noise made Sarah, who was in the seat ahead of him, turn around. "I don't know why you're eating that now," she said. "We're getting supper at the Careys', you know."

Jack glanced over at Alexander, who nodded back. It seemed they were going with Alexander's plan after all.

Jack sighed and took another bite. He remembered Jeb's warning: *You'll all get sick of apples.* But, of course, Jack knew that couldn't happen. They wouldn't be staying long enough, would they?

11
A PROMISE THEY CAN'T KEEP

Frances couldn't believe it: Sherwood, Missouri, was *right there*. And she had figured out Ned's first clue without even getting off the train! She found the page in her *Third Eclectic Reader* where she'd written down the instructions. *You'll have your boot on in the right direction*, the first part read. When she'd spotted that boot sign, she'd felt her guts leap. She was sure it meant that the boot's toe was pointing the way to the treasure. Now all they had to do was get back there.

This revelation took her mind off the very strangeness of the day. This morning, she and Harold had woken up in a shed in an unfamiliar city. Tonight they would be at Reverend Carey's supper table. At least they'd be getting something to eat, Frances thought. And, of course, they'd gotten away from Miss DeHaven. *But what's next?* she wondered.

Which was why it had been so thrilling to see that clue out the window. Maybe that *boot* was the next step. . . .

Her mind was so full she hardly noticed that the train had stopped. It took Harold, tugging on her arm, to bring her back to attention.

"Frances! This is our stop! We're home—" he exclaimed before he quickly stopped himself. "I mean," he said, more softly, "we're *here*."

Frances didn't want to think about what Harold's slip of the tongue had meant. She nodded and took her brother's hand.

Bremerton wasn't much bigger than Whitmore, Kansas, but it struck Frances as older and more settled, with more brick storefronts on its main street. The land here was different, too, Frances noticed. Kansas had been nearly flat—only a few distant bumps on the horizon—and the trees were thin. Here in Missouri, though, there were low, rolling hills that went on for miles like green waves, and instead of a dusty intersection in front of the train depot, as in Whitmore, there was a little square park with old oak trees.

Before long, she and the other kids were sitting cross-legged in the bed of the Careys' hay wagon as it bounced gently along. For most of the drive, they silently took in the new scenery, with the exception of Nicky, who'd had a small coughing fit, and Anka, who softly hummed a song to herself. Even George and Harold seemed to understand that they were to be on their best and quietest behavior now. Frances couldn't help but notice the difference between Jack, who wore a wary expression and shifted uncomfortably in his seat, and Sarah, who kept smoothing her hair and wiping George's chin with her handkerchief.

Reverend Carey steered the horse team onto a smaller road, past a field full of short, scrubby trees. It was the apple orchard, Frances guessed, judging from the way the trees were lined up in neat rows. She remembered Alexander talking about California and how you could pick oranges from the side of the road. This was *almost* as good as that, she thought. For now, at least.

"Which house is yours?" Frances heard Jack ask Mrs. Carey as the wagon approached a cluster of small board-and-batten houses.

"Oh, the sharecropping farmers live there," Mrs. Carey replied. "They work the oat fields."

Reverend Carey turned to look back at the children. "This used to be a plantation," he explained. "My grandfather built it, and my father ran it after he died. He freed the slaves long ago, of course. Now I'm working to free mankind from other evils."

The closer the wagon got, the more Frances could see how small the houses were. Maybe the sharecroppers weren't slaves, Frances thought, but they still looked awfully poor. On the porch of the nearest house were two women, one wringing something into a washtub, the other with a baby on her hip. They nodded hello as the wagon passed.

Sarah was staring so intensely at the women she had to turn in her seat to keep them in her sight.

"Stop it," Frances whispered. "You act like you've never seen black people before."

Sarah turned red. "I have. Just . . . not at the orphanage." Frances remembered that Sarah had never lived anywhere besides the Home for Destitute Children. It was true that there were mostly white children in the New York orphanages—there was a separate home for black orphans in Harlem. Frances and Harold had been on their own in the city before taking refuge at the Howland Mission and Children's Home, and while it had been rough,

Frances realized, at least they'd known early on that there were all kinds of people in the world.

The wagon finally stopped between a white barn and a two-story brick house. The house was old and large but unadorned—to Frances it seemed like a big box with a roof, like the kind of house Harold would draw when he was supposed to be practicing his letters. Behind the house was a tiny clapboard chapel, and a little farther beyond that were the sharecroppers' houses.

"Is that where we're going to live?" George asked loudly as the children climbed out of the wagon. He pointed at the brick house, gazing up at its tall windows.

Reverend Carey paused before answering. "That will be up to you, children. We'll discuss it at supper. But you are all welcome to take a look inside."

George required no further invitation. Frances couldn't believe how quickly he clambered up the front steps. Nicky and Anka and Sarah weren't far behind.

Frances steadied herself and took Harold's hand. Together, they followed Alexander and Jack up to the porch. But instead of going through the door, the boys hung back, their hands in their pockets.

"Aren't you going in?" she asked them.

Alexander shrugged. "Nah."

"It's just a house," said Jack.

Harold pulled on her hand; he wanted to go inside. Truthfully, Frances was curious, too. So they stepped over the polished wood threshold and into the house.

The place was simply furnished, but there were lots of rooms—a sitting room with straight-backed chairs, a study with a big table made of dark wood, and even a schoolroom with a row of desks, their iron legs bolted to the floor. Mrs. Carey, Frances had heard, taught all her children lessons during the winters.

They came to a big kitchen; Olive and Eleanor were already in there, tending to the enormous cookstove. (Frances paused in the doorway for a moment, hoping she could hear one of them call the other by name so she could tell them apart.) The other children were darting excitedly from room to room. "Look in there!" Anka exclaimed, pointing to a doorway off the kitchen.

Frances gasped when she and Harold crossed the threshold. It was a big pantry—shelves filled with gleaming jars of fruit and beans and pickles and at least a dozen barrels and casks lined up along the floor. They had never seen so much food in one place.

Now in a half daze, Frances and Harold climbed the stairs. Most of the second floor was one room, with two rows of beds—six narrow beds with brown woven blankets and plain iron bedsteads. Sarah and George had already chosen their beds; Sarah was smoothing the pillow of hers. "A real mattress again," she sighed.

Frances stared down at the nearest bed. She knew she *should* be happy like Sarah. But all these beds in one place—it was like the orphanage. The last time she'd had a bed like this was at the Howland Mission back in New York. Even then she remembered thinking that she ought to be grateful for a decent place to sleep, but all she ever really felt was trapped. Just one more cot in a row in a room that was locked up at night . . . and now *this* room, it was much smaller. . . .

It was suddenly hard for her to breathe.

Harold squeezed her hand. "Franny, are you all right?"

She took a deep breath. "Harold?" she asked. "Do you want to sleep up here?"

He didn't say anything for a moment, but finally he looked up at her. "We don't have to," he mumbled. "Not if you don't want to."

Frances knelt down to look her little brother in the eye. "We can stay in the barn, you and me," she said. "As long as we're together, that's all that matters, right?"

Harold tried to smile. "Right," he said.

Jack had heard the inside of the house was nice, but he and Alexander were more interested in seeing the rest of the place. For the first time since they left Kansas it seemed to Jack that he and Alexander were really thinking alike. It was a relief to explore the big white barn without squabbling about something.

Alexander had once lived on a farm in Pennsylvania, so he knew what all the equipment and tools were for. He showed Jack the haymow and pointed out the big grappling hooks that were used to move bales of hay. Then he pointed to a corner of the barn. "That'll be a good place to sleep. Enough room for all eight of us."

"Just for tonight, at least," Jack was quick to add. *Then we'll make a run for it, right?* he thought. The thing was, he wasn't so sure all eight of them wanted to sleep there after seeing the house, but he didn't know how to say that to Alexander. So he was relieved when Mrs. Carey called them over to the water pump in order to wash up for supper.

The food was served up on a long table in the backyard, alongside which were benches for the children and seats at the ends for the Reverend and Mrs. Carey. Jack couldn't wait to eat—there was cold ham, and bread with fresh butter, and pickles, and a big platter of apples fried with onions that smelled wonderful.

But first there was the grace. Reverend Carey gave thanks for the food and the safe journey home, then he blessed "the souls who had found the path to temperance." (Jack had asked Frances what *temperance* was—it meant avoiding liquor.) Then the Reverend blessed the orchards and the crops and the sharecroppers, whose shanties they had passed in the wagon. Next he blessed his own children— Jeb and Olive and Eleanor and the three others who were no longer at home but were off doing the Lord's work as missionaries. Then he said, "Bless Alexander and Anka and Frances and George and Harold and Jack and Nicholas and Sarah, who have come to us today. . . ."

This was the longest grace that Jack had ever heard in his life, though he was impressed that the Reverend knew all their names in alphabetical order.

"And may they choose the right path," Reverend Carey continued. Jack wondered what he meant by that.

Once the Reverend had stopped speaking, Mrs. Carey sang "Amazing Grace." Jack was so hungry by now his eyes were crossing, but he had to admit her voice was pretty.

Then it was time to eat. It was all Jack could do not to wolf down the bread, which was cut into thick slices, and gulp down the cold milk that the Carey girls poured into tin cups from a big pitcher. He was full all too quickly, but somehow he found more room once Mrs. Carey brought out two apple pies and began cutting them into slices.

As soon as the pie was finished and the plates collected, Reverend Carey stood and spoke. "Dear children, Mrs. Carey and I know your lives have been hard. We know of the miseries of the city—the factories, the saloons, the poverty. Some of you have had your families torn apart by liquor and other evils. . . ."

It was true that Jack's father spent most of his

pay on whiskey—sometimes Jack's and his brother's wages, too—and it had made things harder. He knew his wasn't the only family affected: One night back in Kansas, Anka had confessed that her mother died from drink. Now he looked over at Anka and saw she was listening intently to Reverend Carey's words, her eyes shining with tears.

"Your new life here will not be easy," the Reverend went on. "You must work to help us and earn your keep. But if you choose to stay here in our home and mind our rules, you will in time become part of our family."

Jack looked across the table to meet Frances's eyes, but he couldn't figure out what she was thinking. Her expression was solemn and calm as she squeezed her little brother's hand. What did that mean?

"Just one more thing," Reverend Carey said. "Our rules are simple, but there is one promise that is very important, especially in light of what happened today at the depot." He looked straight at Jack just then. "Anyone who chooses to live in our house must promise to *never* lie again."

Jack felt a lump in his throat. He lied at the depot just so they could save themselves. He and all the other kids—they lied only when they had to. Besides, half the time grown-ups weren't honest with them.

He and Alexander exchanged a glance. He knew neither of them could make that promise.

"That is what you must agree to in order to live under our roof," the Reverend went on. "No lying, for any reason."

Around him, all the other children were silent. Although someone across the table—Sarah—was nodding in agreement.

It was no surprise to Jack, then, when at dusk Sarah was the first to go inside to stay in the big brick house. Mrs. Carey had gathered the children on the front porch to give them bits of soap to wash up with. Then, if they chose, they could go in and use the basin in the house before heading up to bed.

"I'll sleep in the barn," Alexander told Mrs. Carey.

"So will I," said Nicky. "And also Jack, right?"

Jack said yes, though he couldn't bring himself to look Mrs. Carey in the eye.

She seemed taken aback for a moment, but she said only, "Very well. You can wash up at the pump in the yard."

Anka took her piece of soap and went inside the house. Jack had figured the girls would want to stay in the house. But then George went in, too.

That left only Frances and Harold. "Ma'am, my little brother thinks it would be fun to sleep in a barn," she explained. "And, you know, I ought to look after him."

Jack was relieved that Frances and Harold weren't going inside. Though, from the look on Harold's face, Jack suspected that staying in the barn wasn't really his idea. Mrs. Carey just smiled sweetly, though she looked a little sad.

"Let me at least give you some blankets," she told them. She turned and pulled out some woolen blankets from a trunk just inside the front door and handed them to Jack and Nicky.

Nicky started to say "Thank you," but broke into another coughing fit before he could get out the words. He'd always coughed a little, but he seemed to be having more spells ever since they'd left Kansas, and the dust of the train car and the smog around the depot couldn't have helped any. Jack could hear him wheeze between coughs.

"Oh my goodness," Mrs. Carey said. She took his blanket and wrapped it around his shoulders.

"You'd better not sleep in that musty barn. I've got some mint tea and honey that will help."

Nicky hesitated for a minute. Then another cough came on. "Okay," he said, and Mrs. Carey led him inside. Jack couldn't help but notice her face brighten as she brought another child into the house.

The door swung shut with an efficient click. Jack, Frances, Harold, and Alexander looked around at one another, dumbstruck. Alexander managed a wry smile. "Citizens of Wanderville," he said, "let's head over to the barn."

12
OUTSIDE THE HOUSE

Alexander found a lantern in one of the horse stalls, and Jack was glad to learn that he still had matches in his pocket. After a moment, the lamp was lit, and the four set to work making a corner of the barn comfortable. Frances discovered some feed sacks to put down over the hay bales, and with the blankets on top they had some decent beds.

They stepped back to admire their work. "Not bad for a barn," Frances said.

They heard a sudden laugh from behind them.

"*Not bad?* Why, you've got it looking like a palace!"

Jack turned and saw two figures watching them from the doorway. The woman was the one who'd spoken—the same one Jack had seen standing on her porch with the washtub that afternoon. She wore a faded work dress and a crooked grin. The man was in overalls; he was sunburned and had watery blue eyes.

They were from the sharecropping families, Jack realized. The Reverend had explained that they worked on the Careys' farmland in exchange for a portion of the crops.

"So you're the orphans. Preacher Carey said there'd be a few of you staying in the barn," the man said. As he spoke, more new faces appeared in the doorway—some black, some white. There were about a dozen men, women, and children in all; and they wore worn work clothes and dungarees.

"The name's Clement Bay," said the sunburned man. "I'm the fellow who first welcomes strangers around here." He introduced them to his wife, Ella, and their baby girl, Liza, who was just starting to walk.

The woman with the washtub was named Ora, and she shared a shanty with her son and his wife. "So you got nowhere in the world to go, but you ain't staying in the preacher's big house?" she asked.

Jack shrugged. "I guess."

"They wanted us to promise not to tell lies," Harold said, much to Frances's embarrassment.

Ora laughed deeply. "And you couldn't promise that, could you?"

Harold shrugged. "I guess not. Even though they have a whole room full of jars of jam. But Frances said the barn will be fun."

Jack liked these people. They reminded him of some of the kinder neighbors back in the New York tenements who'd look out for Jack and his brother on days when their father didn't come home and their mother had to work. As he and Frances and Alexander said hello to each of the poor farmers, he glanced around to see if anyone was close to their age. The sharecropper children, though, seemed to be either older teenagers or toddlers and babies.

Alexander must have been looking around for the same reason, because Jack heard him ask Ora, "Is that your grandson over there?"

Jack turned and saw where his friend was pointing. Out past the barn entrance, over by the sharecroppers' houses, a boy stood and watched them. Judging by his build, he seemed to be about ten, but his face looked older somehow. He bent to pick up a rock, aimed, and threw it hard in the direction of the chicken yard, making the birds scatter.

"Oh, that's Eli," Ora said. "He's Moses Pike's boy. And he's *trouble*."

Alexander nodded and began to walk toward the boy. Jack followed. But when Eli saw them coming, he turned on his heels and trudged back to his house.

The sharecroppers went to bed early because their work began at sunrise. "You kids ought to turn in, too, if you got chores," Clement had told them.

Back in the barn, Alexander adjusted the flame lower on the lantern, Jack stretched out on his blanket, and Frances helped Harold unbutton his shoes.

"Do we have to stay here for a long time?" Harold asked.

Frances turned to Jack and Alexander. "That's what I'd like to know."

This did nothing to calm Harold. "Is this like the ranch?" he cried. "Are they going to make us work?" He had one shoe off, and he wobbled on one leg in panic.

His sister took him by the shoulders to steady him. "I think it's different here, Harold." She looked over at the two older boys again. "Right?"

Jack nodded. "The Careys aren't like the Pratcherds. They're not cruel. They mean well, but . . ."

"They just want things to be a certain way," Alexander said.

"I get it—while we're here, we have to go by their rules," Frances said. "But how long are we going to be here?"

"Yes, Alexander, *how long*?" Jack added. The same question had been on his mind all evening. "I thought we were going to leave in the morning and find a train to California!"

"Of course we're still going to California!" Alexander snapped. "It's just a question of when! Now that Nicky's sick, that changes things a bit. We'll just wait until he's better, and we'll talk to the others. . . ." His voice trailed off.

"That's just it," Jack said. "What if the others don't want to leave here?"

"They will," Alexander said firmly.

Frances spoke up just then. "I don't want to go on another train. Not yet . . ."

Jack grinned. "I bet you want to go look for that crazy hobo treasure."

"Maybe!" Frances replied. "I mean, who knows?

There might be something. It's *not* crazy." Her face turned red for a moment, but then she seemed to compose herself. "But . . . really I meant that we should stay away from trains for a while after all that trouble in Kansas City. These orphan trains—they're going everywhere, and some busybody stationmaster could put us on another one. And what if Miss DeHaven is looking for us?"

Harold nodded at that, and Jack had to agree that Frances had a point.

"So you're saying you'd rather go on a wild-goose chase to find Ned Handsome's pot of gold?" Alexander said with a snort.

"I think she's saying," Jack said, looking Alexander in the eye, "that we shouldn't leave until we have a better plan."

"*My* plan got us this far," Alexander replied. "To a place where we're safe and treated decently. Trust me, I'll figure it out from here."

At that, he extinguished the lantern, and the four of them said their good-nights.

Jack lay down facing the barn wall and pulled his blanket around his shoulders. He was beginning to think Alexander didn't have a plan at all. Or that his only plan was to try to stay in charge.

13
A DAY OF WORK

They woke to the noise of roosters and geese. Harold kept giggling at the clucking sounds, but Frances didn't think they were so funny this early in the morning. From the looks of Jack and Alexander, who stumbled out of the barn behind her, neither did they.

She splashed her face with cold water from the pump, then made her way to the yard between the barn and the house, where Mrs. Carey and one of her daughters (Frances thought it might be Eleanor) were setting out hard rolls and mugs of coffee for the sharecropping farmers.

When Mrs. Carey saw Frances, she pulled her aside. "Here's an old dress of Olive's that should fit you," she said, handing her a mug of milk and a bundle. "There's no reason why you should keep wearing boys' clothes."

Frances looked down at the breeches she'd been wearing for the past few days. She'd nearly forgotten that she'd had them on—she'd pulled them off a clothesline back in Whitmore just before they'd escaped.

"Thank you, but it's all right," she said. "I . . . I think I'll keep wearing these for now." Frances thought about all the things she'd been able to do in trousers, like climb the side of a train. "I'd hate to get a nice dress dirty."

Mrs. Carey took the bundle back. "Maybe you'd like to wear it later," she said, her voice hopeful. "And maybe you'd like to come live inside with the other girls soon. Just let me know."

Frances didn't know what to say to that. She gulped down her milk, then mumbled another thank-you and hurried back to the barn.

The morning went by quickly. First, Frances and the boys helped pump and carry water for the horse troughs. Then Jack and Alexander went off to put in fence posts while Frances and Harold tended the big garden. Clement showed them how to pull weeds and look for strawberries to pick. "Don't eat too many," he warned with a wink.

"This is much better than that dumb beet field at the Pratcherds'," Harold said, popping a fat berry into his mouth as they worked. "And everyone's nicer, too."

Her brother was right. Nobody raised his or her voice, or snapped at them, or made threats. The one exception was a stubble-faced fellow named O'Reilly who had a loud, honking voice and a surly temper. He seemed to be the head farmhand, and when he passed the children by the garden he would gripe, "Just what we need! More brats running around!" But Frances was pretty sure they could stay clear of him.

Her favorite job was in the orchard that afternoon, where she and Harold and the older boys were supposed to look through the apple trees and find branches for cutting. Reverend Carey came out from his study to show them how to locate the best branches—the ones with lots of leaves and buds at the tips—and then how to tie a strip of cloth around to mark them.

"You may need to climb the trees," the Reverend said. "That's why you're the best ones for the job."

Later, one of the farmers would come and cut the branches, he explained, and then use the cuttings to grow new saplings, or even graft them onto other trees.

"Why can't the apple trees just grow from seeds?" Jack asked.

"They can, but they won't grow as well, and their fruit won't be good," Reverend Carey replied. "They'll be wild."

"Wild, huh?" Alexander muttered, shoving his hands deep in his pockets.

Frances noticed that the Reverend had a way of making everything sound as if it was important. Like there was a lesson to be learned from apples.

Before long, the four children were making their way down the row of trees, finding one or two branches from each one and tying on the markers. The pace was slow, but the task was strangely satisfying.

"Hey, Frances," Alexander called from the other side of the row. "Did you puzzle out all of Ned's clues yet?" He liked to tease her about her fascination with the hobo treasure, but Frances had a feeling that he, too, was truly curious.

"Just the first one," she said. "But I bet if we were in Sherwood, we'd be able to figure the others out."

"I just want to know what Ned hid away in the first place," Jack said. "Do you think it's money?"

"Gold!" Harold exclaimed. "Silver and rubies!"

"Whatever it is, Ned said we wouldn't need it if we made it to California. So it can't be money," Frances speculated.

"Why not?" Jack asked as he swung down from a tree limb. "Wouldn't we need money in California?"

"We'd need some to *get* there," Frances said. "So we'd have to go to Sherwood first. It's twelve miles away. . . ."

"We'd have to walk there. Sherwood's farther away than Bremerton, and it would take a whole day to get there and back," Alexander pointed out. "And for what? I bet it's just an old pair of boots that Ned left."

"Or an old banjo." Jack laughed. "With the strings broken."

"You're fools, the both of you," Frances replied, but she laughed, too.

They were coming to the end of a tree row and

had reached the edge of the orchard, where there was a fence being built. It was the same one Jack and Alexander had worked on earlier, and now the sharecropper boy named Eli was putting in the rest of the fence posts, while O'Reilly, the surly farmer, barked instructions.

"Set it straight, boy! Push it the other way! No, not that way! Get another post!"

It didn't seem fair to Frances that Eli had to lift the heavy posts when O'Reilly was twice as strong.

"Need help?" Jack called over to Eli. But he only shook his head and looked away. *Stubborn*, Frances thought.

O'Reilly snorted in disgust at the boy. "You're no good. *I'll* do it." He shoved Eli aside and grabbed the fence post. "You go get me some water. It's hot out here!"

Eli ran off toward the barn. In the meantime, the man pushed against the fence post and hit it with his shovel. It became more crooked somehow, which made O'Reilly curse and kick at it.

Eli returned with a pail and dipper, walking right by the tree where Frances and Jack stood. The boy wouldn't look at them, but Frances could see the faintest smile on his face. She glanced down and saw that the pail was almost empty—not enough water to even fill the dipper.

He handed the pail to O'Reilly without a word.

The man's face went red with rage when he picked up the dipper. "What's *this*?" he sputtered.

"*Some* water," Eli said matter-of-factly. Then he turned and ran out of the orchard as fast as he could.

"Can you believe that kid?" Frances heard Jack say as they were walking back toward the house.

O'Reilly had stomped off with the pail, and none of them wanted to be around if he came back. It was late afternoon and they were supposed to be returning for supper anyway.

"That was really something," Frances agreed. "I guess that's what they mean when they say Eli's trouble."

"It's the best kind of trouble," Alexander said.

"Look!" Harold said, bolting ahead of them toward the yard. "There's George and Nicky! And Anka and Sarah! And lemonade!"

Frances ran to catch up. She saw the Careys—the Reverend and Jeb were chipping ice, and Mrs. Carey and the girls were slicing lemons and stirring pitchers at the big table.

Near them stood the other four kids. The first
thing Frances noticed was that they were in fresh
clothes. George's hair was neatly combed, and Sarah
and Anka were wearing dresses that were similar to
the one Mrs. Carey had offered Frances—although,
Frances noticed, theirs weren't as faded. As for
Nicky, he had a strange cloth tied around his neck
and under his shirt. "It's a poultice," he said. He
smelled of camphor, but he was no longer wheezing.

"Nicky is in bed all day," Anka told Frances.
"But the rest of us, we help Mrs. Carey. What do you
do today?"

Frances started to tell her and Sarah about the
orchard and the garden.

"You're in the *fields*?" Sarah said. "I'm never
doing that again. You should come live inside!"

"Well . . . I don't mind being out there," Frances
said. "The orchard is pretty. . . ."

"We made strawberry jam, too," Sarah continued. "Eleanor showed us how."

"Mmm! Did you have jam sandwiches?" Harold
exclaimed. But almost as soon as he said it, he
stopped and looked up at Frances. "I mean . . . that's
nice," he said in a much smaller voice.

Just then, Mrs. Carey handed them glasses of

lemonade. Frances took a sip. It was cold and sweet, but as she swallowed, she could feel a lump in her throat.

"Drink up, dear. And then we'll all go to the chapel," Mrs. Carey told her. "We often end the workday with prayers and reflection."

Frances nodded. "Okay." *Reflection* sounded quiet and nice. It had to be better than the matrons droning their way through the verses of *Pilgrim's Progress* back at the orphanage in New York.

She found Harold, and they made their way to the little clapboard chapel, which had only a few rows of benches inside. The other kids were already there, along with several of the sharecroppers. She and Harold took a seat, and then turned to look for the boys. Alexander came over to their bench and sat down beside them.

"Where's Jack?" Frances whispered.

Alexander motioned toward the door.

Jack was still in the doorway. His shoulders were hunched around his ears and his hands were pushed deep in his pockets. He shook his head and took a step back.

He's not coming in, Frances realized.

She turned the other way to see the Reverend at

the front of the chapel. He seemed to meet Jack's eyes. He nodded, though his face was grim and set. Then he stood up straight and did not look in Jack's direction again.

The Reverend cleared his throat. "Let us pray," he began.

Frances looked back once more, just in time to see Jack leave.

14
AN HOUR OF PRAYER

Jack had asked to be excused from prayers.

"I don't mean that I'm not thankful," he'd told the Reverend. "It's just . . ." He couldn't put it into words. He thought about what happened in the depot the day before, when it looked like he and the others were going to be sent back to Kansas. He'd wished for a way to escape—was that *really* praying? If it was, it was the first time he'd prayed since his brother died. And as it happened, the way to escape had been to lie and say they were with the Careys. Had *that* answer come from praying? Jack didn't know what to think.

He was relieved when Reverend Carey didn't ask for an explanation, though disappointment passed over his face like a cloud.

Jack had been out in the yard for half an hour now, and he was bored. He idly kicked a pebble against the side of the chapel. Even outside he could hear the Reverend's voice, going on about how children were like apple tree boughs. Jack knew he was talking about them—the orphan train kids.

"Let our family be the strong rootstock unto which these boughs may grow," Reverend Carey intoned, followed by a chorus of *Amens*.

That was kind of the Careys, Jack thought, but the last thing he wanted was to be rooted here.

He found another pebble, kicked it as far as he could, and ambled after it. But as he went, he began to hear voices—was there an argument going on in the barn?

"You do what the man says! You fetch the water like he tells you!"

After a few more steps, Jack heard noises that were sickeningly familiar: the thud of fists, followed by the sharp smack of a hand.

He wanted to run, but he turned the wrong way, and that's when he saw a man by the side of the barn with his arm raised to strike, and strike hard. There was a boy at his feet. Eli.

Jack could guess who the man was. He had the

same high forehead as his son, though his brow was slick with sweat and his eyes were wild.

As soon as Eli's father saw Jack, his arm fell slack to his side and he stumbled a little. It was clear he'd been drinking. He shuffled a few more steps and picked up something on the ground behind Eli—a bottle, which he shoved into his pocket.

Mr. Pike glowered in Jack's direction. "It's your lucky day," he told Eli. Then he staggered around the side of the barn and was gone.

Eli brushed dirt from his shirt and wiped his face with his sleeve. Jack came closer and extended a hand to help him off the ground. But Eli hesitated a moment before letting Jack pull him up.

"Are you all right?" Jack asked him.

Eli didn't say anything.

"My father, he would drink, too. . . ."

"Save it for the Reverend," Eli said. He yanked his arm away and stepped back.

From the way the kid felt the side of his mouth as if to check his teeth, Jack knew this wasn't the first time he'd been hit like that.

Jack tried again: "But the Careys . . . they could help you." Didn't Reverend Carey preach against liquor and try to save people who were hurt by it?

"They wouldn't. Not a kid like me," Eli said. "Or my old man."

"What do you mean?" Jack asked. But as soon the words were out, he wished he hadn't said them. Because he knew what Eli had meant: Eli and his father were black.

"I don't need pity from the Reverend anyway," Eli shot back. "Or you." And then he walked off.

The prayers were over now and everyone was trickling out of the chapel. From where Jack stood, he could see the other kids. George and Harold were racing to the water pump; Alexander was telling Anka and Sarah a story; and Frances was helping Nicky fix his neck wrap.

Jack watched as Harold won the race to the water pump. "Let's race back!" Harold shouted. George agreed, but not before he glanced at the house and then down at his clean shirt. He looked nearly as tidy as Sarah and Anka, who stood nearby with Alexander.

"You should've seen O'Reilly's face when he looked in the pail . . . ," Alexander was saying while the girls laughed. Jack knew he was talking about what Eli had done in the orchard.

Jack hung back. He didn't want to tell anyone what had happened after Eli's father found out about the incident.

Just then, Jack saw Ora; she was lugging a heavy cooking pot from the sharecroppers' shanties over to the pump. She smiled as she passed Jack.

"Wait," he said. "Is Eli all right? I saw . . ."

Ora stopped walking and sighed as she set down the pot. "I know what you saw. Moses Pike gets that way with the gin. Eli tries to hide when it happens, but his daddy's temper was too high today."

"Does Mr. Pike always take it out on Eli?" Jack asked.

"I wish it weren't so," Ora said. "But he hasn't been the same since Eli's mama died. A terrible fever she had when Eli was just seven. The boy was sick, too, but he lived. After that, Moses took up drinking."

Jack just nodded. He didn't know what to say.

Ora picked up the cooking pot and looked straight at Jack. "I'm only telling you the story because of what you saw," she said. "You will not repeat it."

"I won't," Jack promised.

Ora went on. "Eli's all right. If he needs anything, he'll come to our place. My son and his wife keep an eye out for him same as I do. As for Eli's daddy, he's sleeping it off now. And *you*—you ought to get back to the Careys." With that, she continued her walk to the pump.

Jack made his way back to the yard of the big house, where it was time to be seated for supper. He found a spot on the bench next to Sarah, who was busy reminding Harold to be quiet while the Reverend said grace.

"We have to show that we're grateful for the food," she explained. "Do you see that pot of delicious chicken stew and dumplings? We're thankful for that, you know. . . ."

"Of *course*," Frances cut in quickly. "Yes, Harold, we should be thankful."

Maybe she wasn't bossing around her little brother as much as she used to, Jack noticed, but he could tell she sure wasn't about to let someone else do it for her.

Harold's eyes were big as he stared at the steaming pot. "Wow. We're really lucky, aren't we?"

"Yes," Jack said quietly. "We're really lucky."

15
WHAT HAROLD FOUND

Frances was glad that there were not too many evening chores, because even after supper, it was still light outside—enough bright sky to last at least another hour—and she wanted to show the other girls the apple orchard. So she and Harold hurried as they took scraps to the pigs and helped stack the dirty dishes.

"Thank you, dear. That will be all." Mrs. Carey stood at the kitchen door and took the last of the plates from Frances. "Sarah and Anka will help me with the washing-up."

"When will they be done?" Frances called after her, but it seemed Mrs. Carey hadn't heard her, and then the door fell shut.

Frances felt stupid waiting on the back steps. All

she wanted was for Sarah and Anka to see the apple trees—to see how pretty they were and how thrilling they were to climb. (Well, when you were wearing breeches, at least.) Then maybe they'd stop giving her pitying looks the way they had at supper tonight.

"What do we do now?" Harold asked.

"Go watch Jack and Alexander chop wood," she said. "I'm going to read until the girls can come back out."

But Harold shook his head. "Let's knock on the door! I want to go in the house and have jam sandwiches! George says they're delicious. . . ."

"*Harold*," Frances growled, pointing toward the barn. "Do as I say. Go."

Finally, Harold ran off toward the barn, while Frances found a decent patch of grass and took out her *Third Eclectic Reader*, turning straight to the page with Ned's instructions. She was trying to memorize them, step by step, in the hopes that she could work out the clues in her head somehow.

Cross an Indian, a saint, and one of our founding fathers was next on the list. What did *that* mean? Frances wondered. You could cross a horse and a donkey and get a mule, but what did you get when you crossed saints and Indians and founding fathers?

It gave her a headache. She tried to think of saints' names: St. John the Baptist, St. Joseph, St. Nicholas, but there had to be *thousands* of those. . . .

She rubbed her eyes and looked up. She could see Jack and Alexander at the woodpile. *Just* Jack and Alexander, though. She looked around the yard and then ran over to the boys.

"Where's Harold?"

Alexander shrugged. "He was here a minute ago."

Jack nodded.

Frances suspected neither of them had been paying attention, since their wood-chopping had turned into some kind of dumb log-balancing contest. "Never mind," she muttered, and ran toward the barn, calling for her little brother. "Harold! Where are you?"

"I'm here!" came his reply.

"What do you mean, *here*?" Frances was beginning to lose patience. *"Where?"*

Harold didn't answer for a moment. And then he called back:

"In Wanderville!"

Behind the barn was a split-rail fence, and just beyond the fence was the place that Harold had found. It was a small, grassy clearing, and at one end stood an old stone chimney. Frances could see a crumbling fireplace at the base, and where part of a wall had been, the remnants of its stone foundation still lay in the grass. There were other bits of wall throughout the clearing, too, including a corner section that stood almost as tall as Harold.

"There was a house here!" he exclaimed. "A hundred years ago, I bet!"

"I don't know if it was that long ago," Frances said, but the stones did look old, with moss and lichen growing over them. It was a beautiful place, and a little mysterious, too.

"And there are apple trees!" Harold pointed all around. The trees looked scruffier than the ones in the orchard, and they weren't in neat rows. "So there's food right here!"

"I think those are wild trees. Reverend Carey said their apples aren't any good," Frances replied. Then, fully appreciating her brother's comment, she added, "Besides, why would we need to find food?"

Harold didn't seem to be listening. Instead, he was walking around the old chimney. "This can be the town square, and over there can be where we sleep. . . ."

"Harold, *no*," Frances said firmly. She didn't want Harold to get too attached to this place. They were going to leave as soon as they had the chance. And the sooner they fled, the sooner they could make their way back to Sherwood and find out what Ned had left them. Even if it wasn't a treasure, it had to be worth *something*, Frances thought. But everyone kept getting distracted here at the Careys'. Especially Harold.

"What do you mean, *no*?" Harold protested.

Frances sighed. "This isn't Wanderville."

"Why not? It can be anywhere. That's one of the laws."

Frances started to tell her brother that they already had a perfectly good place to sleep in the barn, but just then, they heard a voice behind them.

"That doesn't mean this place can't still be Wanderville," Alexander said. He and Jack had climbed over the fence and were looking all around. "This is a great spot." Alexander grinned—a look Frances remembered from the very first day they'd met him in Kansas. "We can rebuild here!" he declared.

"We sure can," Jack agreed.

"We can't live here . . . ," Frances protested.

"But we can call it *home*," Harold insisted.

"He's right," Jack said. Suddenly Frances understood: The Careys' farm was just where they were staying. But she could see it meant something to Harold to have his very own place. This was a way to have both.

"Just one thing, though," Frances said. "The Careys give us meals. So there's no need to steal food."

"You mean *liberate* it?" Harold piped up.

"*No* liberating *or* stealing food!" Frances told her little brother. "Understand?"

"Right," Alexander said. "The second law of Wanderville shall not be enforced. Not unless . . ." He stopped suddenly, and Frances realized they could hear footsteps in the grass, coming closer.

They turned and saw Ora and Ella, Clement's wife. Ella was carrying her baby and Ora had a basket covered by a cloth.

Ora laughed. "I don't suppose it's breaking the law if we offer you children some biscuits, is it?"

Jack was relieved that the sharecroppers had come across Wanderville rather than the Careys. The Reverend wouldn't understand what the place was for. But the poor farmer families were curious about

Jack and his friends—Jack had overheard Clement calling them "the outside orphans"—and seemed to respect them more for deciding to not live in the big house.

Ella and Ora were soon joined by others, including the rest of Ora's family. They brought lanterns, since dusk was coming on. The glow of the flames was matched by fireflies, and suddenly, it felt almost like a celebration.

"It's real peaceful over here," Clement said. "It's good to have a place to go that's all your own."

"This was an old settlers' place," Ora told the children, motioning to the crumbled walls. "Nice to see it being settled again."

Harold was excitedly showing everyone around Wanderville. "This is the hotel," he said, pointing to one corner. "And the fireplace is the courthouse. . . ."

"Can little Liza have a castle?" Ella asked, jiggling her baby. "And for me, a fancy parlor with silk curtains."

"Right there!" Harold said, pointing at a grassy spot a few feet away.

Jack sensed someone watching them from the fence. He turned and saw Eli.

"Hi . . . ," Jack called out, but the boy ignored

him and wouldn't even look in his direction. Then finally, he made his way over to Ora and took a biscuit to eat. He hung back behind a section of wall and watched Harold build his imaginary houses.

Meanwhile, Clement had brought over some rope and was working with Alexander to build a swing from one of the sturdier trees. Baby Liza and Ora's grandchild were toddling through the grass, trying to grab fireflies.

"We should have some music out here sometime," Ella said. "Some singing."

Frances was finally smiling, and Jack felt better, too. He watched as Harold showed Ora where her mansion was.

"I get a big gold bathtub," she insisted.

Then Harold spotted Eli. "Where do you want your house?" he asked him.

Eli just shook his head. "I'm not playing this game."

"It's not a game; it's Wanderville," Harold said. "And you don't have to have a house, either. You can have something else. What do you want?"

Jack held his breath as Eli seemed to consider the question. At last the boy nodded. "A train that goes anywhere," he said. He grinned at Harold.

Then he slipped away over the fence.

16
A WELL-DRESSED VISITOR

Jack wondered when Alexander would mention leaving the farm again, but he couldn't quite bring himself to ask. It had already been a week, and things had settled into a routine. Jack and Alexander and Frances and Harold helped in the orchards and did other odd jobs, like whitewash the front fence. The tasks varied enough that they didn't get weary of the work, though on hot afternoons things could get slow.

From what Jack had heard, the other four children had plenty to do inside the house: canning jam and pickles in the kitchen to store for the winter, and folding leaflets that the Reverend gave out at lectures. Sarah said the Reverend himself stayed in his study most of the day, writing sermons and letters to newspapers about the problems liquor caused in the world.

All the children were together only at prayer time now. At suppertime Mrs. Carey would give the "barn kids" a basket of sandwiches and leave Jack and Alexander and Frances and Harold on their own. So then, in the summer evening light, they would climb over the split-rail fence to the place they now called Wanderville. Sometimes they were too tired from the day's work to do anything but sit and eat, but it was still good. Sometimes Jack thought that spending time there was just as important as eating supper. Maybe more.

Today Mrs. Carey said it was too warm to be inside the house *or* out in the orchard, so she put all eight children to work shelling pole beans and husking corncobs on the front porch.

Jack couldn't complain. It was *hot*, even in the mornings now. He'd taken to dampening his shirt at the water pump to stay cool. Even Frances had traded in her boys' breeches for a work dress—"Just for today," she'd said. Which was just as well, Jack thought, since on their days working in the orchard she'd become the best climber. But now the sun was too heavy to go out there.

As he peeled the corncobs, he was glad to have such a light task, though he knew that others on the farm weren't as fortunate. Already, both O'Reilly and Mr. Pike had walked by the porch calling for Eli, who had slipped away from his work in the fields.

"I know that boy is hiding," Mr. Pike had muttered. "I'll pound him to mush."

O'Reilly snorted at that. "But you best make sure he can still work, Moses," he warned. "You're both just lucky things aren't the way they were in the old days around here. . . ."

Jack had winced when he heard that and looked over at the Careys. The Reverend sat in a rocking chair, studying a Bible with print so small that he had to lean forward and trace the lines with his finger. Mrs. Carey was busy pouring a glass of lemonade for Harold. If they'd heard the men talking, they gave no indication. He hoped Eli had a good hiding place, at least.

As the afternoon wore on, the Carey girls came out to join the group on the porch with their sewing, and Jeb brought out his books.

Jack was relieved that the Reverend was so occupied with his Bible. Jack still hadn't attended a prayer session, and he had a feeling that Reverend Carey wanted to talk to him about that. But everyone had fallen quiet in the July heat. Quiet enough that they were able to hear the wagon coming up the road.

"I suppose that's the mail," Mrs. Carey said. "Frances and Jack, you can run down to the front fence and fetch it from Mr. MacDonald so he doesn't have to drive all the way up here."

"Can I go, too?" Nicky asked. He wasn't wearing the poultice cloth anymore.

"Yes, but don't run too hard," Mrs. Carey replied.

Jack felt a little sorry for Nicky, who had been a pretty tough kid before his wheezing got bad. Now he had to ask permission to run to the fence.

The three of them headed down to meet the postman. But it wasn't Mr. MacDonald and his mail wagon; it was a sleek black buggy with a single driver, and it stopped as soon as it reached the fence.

"Hello, *children*," said the driver. She wore a straw hat tied down with a scarf, and in any other circumstance, Jack would have thought her very pretty.

Except, of course, that she happened to be Miss DeHaven.

She stepped down from the buggy and motioned to Nicky to hitch the horse team to the fence. Nicky obeyed, his hands shaking, and Jack could hear him taking gulps of air.

"I imagine you're *enjoying* yourselves here," she said to them. Her eyes fell on Frances in her borrowed dress. "I *knew* you weren't a boy when I saw you at the depot," she hissed. "I remember you from the train from New York." She turned to Jack. "You, too."

She began to walk up to the front porch of the house. Jack and Frances exchanged stunned looks. *What is she doing here?* Jack wanted desperately to run ahead to warn the others, to hide—to do *any-thing*. But he could hear Nicky trying not to wheeze, and they had to make sure he was all right. Frances took Nicky by the arm, and then the three of them followed Miss DeHaven toward the house.

As they walked, Jack could hear Frances almost stomping, and he felt his own hands curling into angry fists. What was the use in staying with the Careys if they weren't safe from Miss DeHaven?

Despite the wilting heat, Miss DeHaven was immaculately dressed, and her SCA&R badge stood out against her crisp white shirtwaist. At the sight of her, all the kids on the front steps stood and parted like the Red Sea to let her pass. When she reached the porch, she handed Mrs. Carey a calling card.

"Good *afternoon*, Mr. and Mrs. Carey," she sang. "I'm here to check on the *children*."

"That would be *Reverend* Carey," Mrs. Carey corrected. "And I beg your pardon, but I don't know what you mean." The Reverend had come over to stand behind his wife, and he nodded in agreement.

"I think you know *very well* I mean the orphans who were placed with you in Kansas City last week," Miss DeHaven replied. "As a representative of the Society for Children's Aid and Relief, it is my duty to make sure these children aren't causing *problems*."

Reverend Carey narrowed his eyes. "The children live *here*. If there are any problems, they will be handled by Mrs. Carey and myself. Not by some meddling 'society.'"

"Of *course* they will," said Miss DeHaven. "But eight children is a lot to take in, and *these* children were *quite* troublesome at their previous placement in Kansas. I have reports of stealing, property damage, vandalism, vicious attacks. . . ."

Jack had to admit that taking the Pratcherds'

wagon *was* stealing. And maybe property damage, too. But they'd needed to escape.

Miss DeHaven went on: "It's hardly a surprise when you consider these children came from the streets of New York, where they lived amid crime and filth, and never learned right from wrong."

Mrs. Carey straightened up. "Miss DeHaven, my husband and I have faith that people—children—can change their ways if they are shown the right path. . . ."

The Reverend broke in, using what Jack now recognized as his sermon voice. "And we will *not* hear such words of judgment spoken in our own house!"

Between Miss DeHaven's accusations and Reverend Carey's thunderous response, Jack could hardly breathe. The other kids stood almost frozen.

After Reverend Carey's outburst, Miss DeHaven just smiled and tucked a lock of hair behind one ear. "I *do* hope I haven't *offended* you. I am *ever so glad* it's not necessary to place any of these children *elsewhere.*"

Jack got the sense that Miss DeHaven meant exactly the opposite of all those sentiments.

"But if the situation ever changes," she added, with a look in Jack's direction, "you have my card."

"And *you* tell your society to leave our family alone!" the Reverend boomed.

By then Miss DeHaven was already striding back to her buggy. A few moments later, she was driving off.

The Reverend looked at Miss DeHaven's calling card. "Meddling spinster," he muttered. He slapped the card down on the porch rail and stormed inside, followed by Mrs. Carey.

Jack was glad that the Careys didn't want to cooperate with Miss DeHaven. He hadn't wanted to stay on the farm—still didn't—but what choice did they have now? They were all safer here than traveling out on their own. Still . . . while the Wanderville behind the barn was good enough for the time being, Jack couldn't help but wonder if there was another Wanderville out there—in California, maybe—one they had yet to build. Maybe Frances felt the same way about Ned's treasure—that it was out there, waiting to be found. If only they weren't stuck here . . .

Just then Jack felt someone nudge his shoulder. It was Jeb Carey.

"Did . . . did you really do all those things in Kansas like the lady said?" Jeb asked excitedly. "Vandalism and all that?"

"Now, Jeb," said either Olive or Eleanor, "you know that's a rude question."

Jack walked over to the far corner of the porch, away from Jeb and the others, to get a better view of the front gate and the road. Not only were they going to have to stay at the Carey farm, he realized with a sinking feeling, but they were going to have to stay on their best behavior.

He stared out at the road. After a few moments, though, he heard a soft shuffling noise just beyond the porch. He looked over the railing and saw Harold—just out of sight of everyone else—crouching on the ground with a glass of lemonade. He was looking into the space under the porch.

"I brought you some more lemonade," he heard Harold whisper to someone.

Jack watched as Eli crawled out from under the porch and took the drink from Harold. He downed it quickly and handed the glass back to Harold with a grateful nod. Then he ducked out of sight.

17
THAT NIGHT IN WANDERVILLE

Frances noticed that Jack came to the prayer session that afternoon. He hesitated only slightly at the door before sitting down next to Frances and Harold.

"I know you're not much for praying," Frances whispered to him. "But you might not mind when the Reverend plays the fiddle."

It was true that the music was Frances's favorite part of prayer time—the simple hymns and the sweetly sad notes that Reverend Carey would play. Her mother—Frances still called her Aunt Mare—used to sing some of those songs when Harold was a baby. Back when Aunt Mare was still around, that was.

Still, the melodies were a comfort, and today Frances's nerves needed soothing. She kept thinking of the look Miss DeHaven had given her when she arrived at the house. Later, after the woman had left, Frances had sneaked a look at Miss DeHaven's calling card, which read:

MISS LILLIAN MERIWETHER DEHAVEN

AGENT, SOCIETY FOR CHILDREN'S AID AND RELIEF

PARK AVENUE, NEW YORK CITY

Somehow, Miss DeHaven's name in print made her even more real and awful. Why had she come? *Eight children is a lot to take in*, she'd said. She must have thought that the Careys would change their minds about having all the children stay. And then, Frances realized, Miss DeHaven would have been more than happy to take the kids and "place them elsewhere." Frances was sure that whatever place Miss DeHaven had in mind wasn't a good one.

The Reverend began to play "The Sweet By-and-By," and it helped remind Frances that at least they were safe here at the farm. She'd even said as much to Harold today, after Miss DeHaven left.

"Don't worry," she'd told her brother. "We have a place to sleep and food to eat. And we've all stayed together, haven't we?"

But as she'd said it, her own voice in her ears didn't sound very certain, and Harold had only managed a tight little smile in response.

Maybe it was because the sky was still so light that evening, or perhaps it was because of the strange events of the day, but all the children were allowed to eat supper outside and then play afterward.

"Go on," Mrs. Carey told the four who slept in the house. "Get some fresh air now that it's cooled down a bit."

Frances's heart leaped. "Finally!" she said, grabbing Sarah's hand and motioning to Anka. "Come on!" She began to lead the girls around the side of the barn. Jack and Alexander were doing the same with Nicky, and Harold was leading George. Frances couldn't help but notice how excited her brother looked, his face the brightest it had been all day.

"Where are we going?" Sarah asked as they reached the rail fence. "We can't leave the farm."

"We're not going far!" Alexander replied as he vaulted the fence.

"It's just over here!" Harold added.

And then they were all in the grassy clearing. No one spoke at first.

"What's this, an old chimney?" George asked, peering up at the stone structure.

"No, it's the courthouse," Harold insisted. "Can't you see?"

"There used to be a house here?" Nicky asked, nudging a bit of old wall with his foot. "That's interesting."

"So what was it you were going to show us?" Sarah asked Frances.

"Just . . . this place," Frances said, though she really wanted to blurt out, *Don't you see it? It's Wanderville!* "It's just the place where we go. Kind of like the place in Kansas." She was hoping Sarah and Anka would understand what she meant, but they just stood there, and Anka kept glancing back at the fence where they'd come in. So did Nicky.

"It's getting dark," Anka said. "We go inside soon."

"Olive is reading *Treasure Island* to us," Sarah added.

"We'll tell you the story when she finishes," Nicky offered.

"Oh, okay," Alexander said, looking over at Jack, who just shrugged. "Good night, then."

And so, the four children who slept in the house

waved goodbye from the fence. Frances waved back, then reached over and gave Harold's hand a squeeze. She didn't want him to feel bad that George didn't want to play.

But Harold only said, "They're silly. They didn't even notice the rope swing."

"Everyone knows a swing's a lot better than *Treasure Island*," Jack said.

Alexander looked truly glum. "Is it really better? I don't even know. . . ."

"Of *course* it's better, you dumb lug!" Jack grinned and grabbed the rope, then made a running leap toward Alexander, who began to laugh. Frances noticed that the boys hadn't quarreled since they'd found Wanderville again; that was certainly a relief.

"Hey, look," said Harold. "Eli's still here." He pointed to the tall corner section of the wall. There was the sharecropper boy, standing behind the wall.

"What do you mean, *still* here?" Frances asked. "Has he been here this whole time tonight?"

Harold nodded. "I told him he could come when . . . when I saw him today." He looked down quickly. "He was hiding. I promised him I wouldn't say where."

Frances shook her head. "It doesn't matter now."

"Eli?" Jack called. "Come on over."

Eli didn't say anything, but his eyes were drawn to the rope swing.

"You can try the swing," Alexander added.

The boy still didn't speak, but a small smile began to play across his face. He stepped closer, into the clearing.

Just then, they heard a voice by the fence. *"Elijah Pike!"*

It was Eli's father. He knocked aside one of the fence rails as he stormed over.

"En't no time for playing. Been looking for you all day. You got work!" he bellowed. He grabbed Eli by the wrist and yanked his arm. "You hear me?" His words sounded thick, and Frances could smell the liquor even from where she was standing. He shook Eli's arm hard.

"Hey!" Alexander called out suddenly. "Don't— don't thrash him."

Mr. Pike looked up and glared. As he did, Eli twisted his arm free and ran over to the fence.

"Mind your own troubles," Mr. Pike growled at Alexander before he turned and went after Eli. Soon they were both out of sight.

The children didn't say anything for a moment.

Frances's whole body had been tensed, as if ready to run herself. Finally, she let out a breath and pulled Harold closer to her side. Jack and Alexander still stood staring at the fence, fists clenched. At last, they relaxed a little when they heard only silence coming from the direction of the sharecroppers' shanties.

"I hope Mr. Pike doesn't come back here," Frances whispered.

Jack nodded. "But maybe Eli will."

18
THE ACCUSATION

Jack was the first one up the next morning. He was starting to actually like getting up at first light. At the pump, he combed his hair back with wet fingers and then took a long drink of cool water while he watched the sunlight spread through the sky behind the orchard. *If we have to stay here awhile,* he thought, *it might be all right.*

The four of them were getting so used to their chores that they'd gotten into a routine of things to talk about to help pass the time.

Alexander liked to talk about plans for Wanderville. "I bet that once we get some hammocks up, and a better rope swing, the other kids will want to spend time there," he said as they tended the garden.

"*Yes!*" Harold said excitedly. "Especially George.

And we can have Ella and Clement and Ora come over, too." He wanted to teach them the Big Rock Candy Mountain song that the hoboes had taught them.

Frances liked to talk about Ned's treasure directions. "One of the clues is 'a house with blue eyes that are always shut,'" she said as they worked in the orchard. "Do you suppose by 'eyes' he means windows?"

Truthfully, the idea that a hobo would have treasure somewhere was beginning to seem pretty silly to Jack. But there wasn't harm in hearing Frances talk about it.

Sometimes they all wondered how Quentin and Lorenzo were doing in their new life riding the rails.

"Do you think they've lost any fingers yet?" Harold wondered. "I hope not."

"Harold!" Frances said. "Don't talk about such things!"

Jack knew Quentin could be tough, and he liked to think that he and Lorenzo were all right. He hoped they could find work in an orchard just like this one when it was time to harvest the apples. He looked around at the trees, their fruit starting to form. It wouldn't be long now. . . .

Reverend Carey's voice interrupted Jack's thoughts. *"Children!"* The minister and his wife marched up the orchard aisle toward them, their faces stern. No, more than stern, Jack realized—they were furious. And Jack noticed the Reverend had a tree bough in his hand.

"To the barn!" the Reverend roared. "All four of you!"

Reverend Carey's fiddle was missing. According to Mrs. Carey, it had vanished from the cabinet in the chapel.

"That's where it's always been kept," she said. "And we put it there last night after the prayer session. Now it's gone. I don't think we need to tell you that fiddle is important in our family."

"Who stole it?" The Reverend paced the barn floor. The four children had been ordered to stand in a line while the Reverend walked up and down their row, stopping to study their faces for signs of guilt.

"We trusted you," Mrs. Carey said bitterly. "We've never had any kind of problems with stealing around here. Until today."

Jack's guts were in knots. He thought about what Miss DeHaven had told the Careys about the children yesterday—that they were "trouble." What if the Careys were starting to believe her? All because of the fiddle. What had happened to it? Could it have been misplaced?

He exchanged confused looks with Alexander and Frances. Frances had turned pale—Jack was sure she was as upset about the fiddle disappearing as she was about being accused of stealing it.

"Who is responsible?" the Reverend cried. "Step forward!"

Jack tried to catch Harold's eye, but the seven-year-old was staring down at the floor and shifting his feet. *Oh, no,* Jack thought.

Alexander noticed how Harold was acting, too. He nudged Jack and gestured toward himself, as if to say, *I'll step forward.*

Jack shook his head and made his own motions: *No, I'll do it.* But Alexander just glared at him, as if Jack were trying to show him up somehow. Jack's face grew hot: They hadn't argued in days, but now they couldn't agree about a thing like *this*?

The Reverend's face was getting redder. "Will no one answer?" He took a deep breath and clenched his fists so hard the bough in his hand began to bend. *"Who took it?"*

"It was me," declared a voice.

The voice belonged to a boy, but not Harold or Alexander.

Eli stepped out from a stall where he'd been hiding. "It was me," he said again. "I took the fiddle."

19
A FIDDLE AND A FIGHT

Frances watched as Eli went over to the corner of the barn where the children slept and pulled the fiddle out from under a blanket. Then he handed it to Mrs. Carey without a word. He simply stood there, quiet and still in a way that seemed almost defiant.

"Have you anything to say for yourself?" the Reverend demanded. He was still clutching the bough.

The boy stayed silent.

"Nothing at all?"

Eli shook his head.

At that, the Reverend took hold of Eli's collar with his free hand. He looked over at the other four children. "Consider this a lesson to you, too," he told them. "For every misdeed there is a punishment."

"We are not running a boardinghouse for thieves," Mrs. Carey added.

She grabbed Eli's arm for good measure, though he showed no sign of resistance. Then the couple marched him out of the barn, through the yard, and up the back steps into the house. The children didn't dare speak until the door slammed shut.

"What happened?" Frances cried. She turned and looked at her little brother. She'd had a terrible feeling about the way he'd been shifting nervously a minute ago, just before Eli spoke up. And now he was acting the same way again.

"Do you have something to tell us, Harold?" Alexander asked.

"Yes," Harold said softly. "It was really me who took the fiddle. I mean . . . I liberated it. For Wanderville."

Frances wanted to shake him. "Didn't we tell you not to do that? Not to steal things this time?" She'd never really approved of the second law of Wanderville, which declared that they could take things they needed, even when it meant stealing them.

"I thought you said not to steal food, that's all," Harold said. "Not other things we needed."

"Maybe I should have made that clearer," Alexander said, looking a little guilty himself.

"Yeah, you should have," Jack muttered. Alexander glared at him.

Here we go again, Frances thought. But she had to ignore their brewing quarrel to turn back to Harold. "But why on earth did you think we needed the fiddle?"

"Because we needed to have music in Wanderville, so . . ." Harold's eyes began to fill up and his voice broke. "So that George and the other kids would want to be there again."

Even in her anger Frances could sense how left out her brother felt. "Well, what's done is done," she said, wiping Harold's tears with her sleeve.

"Why did Eli say he stole it?" Harold wondered, still sniffling.

"I don't know," Alexander said. "I was going to step forward and take the blame so Harold wouldn't get thrashed."

"No, *I* was," Jack replied.

"Oh, so *you're* the leader of us now?" Alexander shot back.

"Is that all you care about?" Jack retorted.

The two faced each other, fists at their sides.

"Stop it!" Frances shouted. "Neither of you stepped forward! *Eli* did! And if you two would stop quarreling for one minute, you would remember why!"

The boys stopped glaring at each other and turned to look at Frances.

"To save Harold, and to save *us*!" Frances cried. "Not just from a thrashing, but from being branded as the criminals Miss DeHaven says we are! The Careys didn't believe her, but if it had been Harold who'd been caught stealing today . . ."

She couldn't bring herself to finish the sentence, but she knew Jack and Alexander were thinking the same thing: *We would have been sent away with Miss DeHaven.*

"Eli must have known," Jack said. "He must have known we had more to lose from being caught."

Frances squeezed her brother's shoulder. "It was a brave thing that he did."

"He's my friend," Harold said quietly. "I think maybe he's our friend, all of us."

"I think so, too," Frances said. She looked across the yard to the house, to the door where Eli had been taken. She suddenly got an awful, shivery sensation from staring at that closed door.

No one said anything for a moment until Alexander spoke up, his voice hushed.

"What do you suppose is happening to him now?"

20
ELI'S FATE

The next morning Eli wasn't working in the oat field the way he usually did. Jack checked the orchard fence, too, but he wasn't there digging posts, either. Jack felt deeply uneasy as he walked back over to the garden, where his three friends were working.

"Did you go by his place?" Alexander asked after Jack had told them.

"He wasn't there," Jack reported. The door of the shanty had been wide open, which had made Jack worry that the Pikes had left in the night. But he'd crept up to the doorway to peer inside, into the shanty's only room. There he'd seen Mr. Pike, asleep in a chair with a bottle on the floor next to him. Eli was nowhere to be found.

"What if he's still at the Careys' house?" Frances

wondered. "Could they have kept him there this whole time?"

"Like a prisoner," Harold said with a shudder.

Last night the prayer session had been extra short. Then, when Mrs. Carey brought a basket of food out to the barn, Harold had piped up and asked where Eli was.

"He's being punished, of course," she'd said. "And you will not ask any more questions about him."

But they wouldn't stop wondering: *What was he going through?*

All morning, as they worked in the garden, they kept looking up at the house.

"Maybe Eli's in the schoolroom," Frances said.

Alexander took a deep breath. "Schoolroom?"

Frances nodded. "It sure looked like the kind of room where punishment happens."

"I'll bet," Alexander muttered. Alexander had told Jack once that he'd had a teacher at school who'd flogged him with a switch.

Now Jack couldn't stop thinking of that tree bough in the Reverend's hand. The minister was a tall man; his arms looked wiry and strong. He didn't seem to Jack to be violent, but he clearly had a strict sense of right and wrong, and believed that harsh discipline was sometimes necessary. But how far would he go to punish Eli?

Ever since they had come here, Jack made sure to remember how different the Careys' farm was from the ranch in Kansas. But then he saw how O'Reilly liked to shove Eli—and some of the other sharecropper kids, especially the black ones—and he didn't understand how Reverend Carey could let his employee carry on like that. Jack tried telling himself it wasn't so bad. But lately he'd gotten to thinking: If you set strict-enough rules and punished enough folks, would it just make you turn mean at some point? Suppose that had happened with O'Reilly, and maybe even the Pratcherds, too. Did that mean—and *this* was what Jack wondered about, even though he hated to think about it—*did that mean it could happen to the Reverend?*

Jack turned so that he couldn't see the big brick house. But Alexander kept looking. "Which window is the schoolroom?" he asked Frances.

She stood on her toes and looked. "Well, the kitchen is that first window, and then a parlor on the other end. . . ." She pointed to a small, high first-floor window in the middle. "That one. That must be the schoolroom."

"It's so high." Jack glanced around. "We'd have to stand on something to see in."

"Like that wheelbarrow," Alexander said, motioning to the one at the edge of the garden.

"Exactly like that wheelbarrow," Jack replied with a grin.

They needed to wait until the workday was nearly over so that they wouldn't look suspicious sneaking over to the house. The Reverend would be going out to lead the prayer session by that time, too.

So when the afternoon shadows started to grow long, the three of them began to slowly push the wheelbarrow toward the house, taking care to roll only a little at a time so that the noise of the rusty front wheel wouldn't attract the attention of O'Reilly, who sometimes threatened to "report" the kids "for being a nuisance."

Finally, they were close enough to the house that they had to crouch down and hide behind the wheelbarrow when the back door opened.

"There's the Reverend now," Frances whispered. "Let's go—quick."

They pushed the wheelbarrow the rest of the way until it was under the window. Alexander held the handles steady, then Frances and Harold sat on one side of the little wagon bed to balance the weight while Jack stood on the other. Perched on the edge of the wheelbarrow, Jack could get just enough of a grip on the windowsill to lift himself up and see inside.

He was almost afraid to look, though. Sometimes it didn't matter that folks like the Careys weren't as cruel as the Pratcherds. When grown-ups were mad enough at you, it could all be the same in the end. But Jack had come this far, so he took a deep breath and pulled himself up to the window, which was partway open. Jack tried to open it wider, but it was locked in place, with only a few inches of space to let in air. Not even Harold could climb in there.

He saw a row of desks in the schoolroom, just as Frances had described. Eli was sitting in the very front one, looking uncomfortable, as if the desk were an iron trap that had somehow captured him. He was all by himself in the room, with a pen in his hand and a sheaf of smudged pages in front of him. He looked up at Jack, stunned. Then he got up from his desk and came closer to the window.

"Are you all right?" Jack whispered. "Did they give you a hiding?"

Eli shook his head. Jack was glad to see he didn't have any bruises or shiners. Still, he looked very tired, though there appeared to be a cot for sleeping in the corner. In front of his desk was a big table with a few crumbs left. *At least they're feeding him,* Jack thought. But then he noticed the tree bough that also sat on the table, and his eyes widened.

Eli saw Jack's reaction. "Preacher Carey sat me down here yesterday and gave a lecture," Eli said. He nodded at the bough. "It was all about that tree branch and how it needs the tree and stuff."

Relief flooded through Jack. The Reverend hadn't hit Eli with the branch—he'd used it to talk about salvation. "But why are you still here?" he asked.

Eli held up a small book. Jack could see the title: *Sermons for Children, On Subjects Suited to Their Tender Age.* "Reverend says there's a sermon about stealing in this book, and I have to copy it fifty times. Trouble is"—Eli turned to make sure the door to the room was still closed—"I ain't been to school since my mama died. So I'm not so good at writing."

Jack saw that the handwriting on Eli's pages was crooked and strange, the letters misshapen. It was taking him a long time just to scribble out one line. "Doesn't Reverend Carey know that you can't write?" Jack asked.

"I ain't telling him."

"Why not?"

"'Cause then I'll be in trouble for missing school," Eli said. "I started skipping to go help in my pa's field on days when he was drinking. 'Cause we'd have no place to live if our crop didn't come in."

Jack was beginning to realize that even though Eli wasn't being hurt, he was in a tough spot. It could be days before his punishment was over.

"That little Harold kid better thank me for saving his hide," Eli added.

"He will," Jack said. "But . . . why did you say you took the fiddle?"

"Because if they sent you away," Eli said, "I wouldn't be able to visit Wanderville with you."

Just then, he felt a tug on the back of his shirt. "Jack! Someone's going to see us out here!" Frances whispered loudly. "You'd better get down."

Jack realized it was almost time for the prayer session. He waved to Eli and lowered himself back down to the ground. Alexander, Frances, and Harold looked to him expectantly.

"Eli's all right," he told them.

"Thank goodness!" Frances exclaimed, while Harold nodded excitedly.

"And he wants to come to Wanderville."

Alexander's face lit up. "He does?"

"Yep," Jack said. But in his head he added: *If he ever gets out of that schoolroom.*

21
ANOTHER PUNISHMENT

For some reason the evening prayers were canceled.

"Reverend Carey has some business to attend to," Mrs. Carey told Frances and the other three children. She handed them a basket for supper.

Frances peered inside the basket—there was fried chicken and bread and a whole apple pie. "Thank you."

"Just bring the basket back tomorrow as usual," Mrs. Carey said. "You all worked so hard today I bet you'll go straight to bed after supper."

Frances couldn't help but notice that this remark sounded almost like a command. Mrs. Carey seemed anxious somehow, too. But Frances kept these thoughts to herself as they returned to the barn.

"I'm glad Eli didn't get a licking," Alexander said as they ate their meal.

"Me, too," Jack said. "And maybe the Reverend will see he's a good kid and will want to help his father stop drinking."

"Then he can come to Wanderville with us," Harold said. He put down his chicken drumstick and looked up at Frances. "Can we go over there now?"

"Well . . ." Frances hesitated. Something about Mrs. Carey's tone had made her wonder if it was better to stay where they were. But after the uncertainty of the past couple of days, Frances longed to go back to her favorite place. "Why not?" she said finally. "We can bring the pie."

"That's a fine idea," Alexander said.

The sky was turning a soft pink as they stepped out the back of the barn. Frances looked down at the pie she was carrying. "We should share this with Ora and Clement and their families," she said. The others agreed, so they turned to walk along the fence over to the sharecroppers' homes.

They came to a big shed where they heard voices. "Maybe Clement's in there," Jack reasoned. They went in and looked around, but nobody was inside.

The late-afternoon light streamed in through the wide spaces between the planks on the wall.

The voices were coming from outside—from the other side of the shed, near a back gate that led to the woods. Not Clement's voice, but other men's voices, and Frances could see silhouettes against the slatted sunlight.

"Frances?" Harold's whisper was hoarse with fear. Frances set the pie down and pulled her brother close.

The sounds of thumps and thuds and shuffling feet weren't noises from work, but from violence. At first Frances thought it was two men fighting. But the sounds of struggle were coming from only one man, she realized. A man who was being shoved and kicked and hit.

She looked over at Jack and Alexander, who looked just as scared as she did. Jack put his finger to his lips and crept over to peer through one of the cracks in the side of the shed. Alexander did the same. Frances slipped her hand over Harold's mouth to make extra sure he'd stay quiet. Then they found a spot in the wall to peer out.

The man being beaten was Moses Pike—Eli's father. He clung to one of the gateposts, his face swollen and bloody. The farmhand named O'Reilly stood before him, his sleeves rolled up and his expression cold.

Frances could feel Harold step back from the wall. She let him bury his face against her side and hugged him closer. The sight made her sick, too, but she kept watching.

Mr. Pike tried to stand taller, but he clutched his side in pain. "I . . . don't . . . understand," he managed to say.

"Just following orders, Pike," O'Reilly said. "Eli needs to mind his elders."

"He's my boy," Mr. Pike said through ragged breaths. "I'll . . . handle it myself. . . . Why won't you let me?"

O'Reilly didn't answer, and after a moment, Frances realized he wasn't the one Mr. Pike was speaking to. Someone else was there, standing off to the side just beyond Frances's field of vision. Another man.

"It's my land," he said. "And these are my rules."

As Reverend Carey spoke, he stepped into view. His coat was off, his shirtsleeves rolled. "I won't strike Eli," he continued. "But someone had to take the blows for what he's done. And when he's finished with his punishment, you'd better mind that boy and keep him away from my family."

Frances felt dizzy and stepped back from the wall. Jack and Alexander did, too. None of them wanted to see any more. But Frances couldn't blot out the image of the Reverend as he had just appeared—still rubbing his fist from the blows. She couldn't forget the blood on his shirt.

Frances hardly needed to pull Harold along as she ran out of the shed. They flew together, the two older boys right behind. Frances heard only the sound of her own panicked breathing, like terrible waves crashing in her head.

22
A TALE OF TWO APPLES

They ran to Wanderville. It was the only place that felt safe.

The fading daylight filtered through the trees as the four of them sat in the soft grass in the clearing. Jack knew they were all thinking the same thing he was.

Harold was the first to voice it. "Is Reverend Carey a bad man?" he asked.

Frances paused a moment before answering. "Remember how we told you the Careys had lots of rules?" she said. "Well . . . I-I guess there are some rules we didn't know about until now." Her voice was shaky, and she picked at the grass as she spoke.

Alexander was silent, sitting with his back to the rest of them, motionless except for the deep breaths he took. Jack, meanwhile, sat with his shoulders tensed, his elbows on his knees. He wanted to curl himself up tight and block all the thoughts that were beginning to burn inside.

He remembered what Eli had said the first time they'd spoken—that the Reverend wouldn't help a black kid the way he helped others. *The problem isn't just that the Careys have rules*, Jack thought. *It's that they have different rules for different people.*

"And we shouldn't break those rules, right?" Harold said. "We'll be fine as long as we follow them, right? As long as we're good?" His voice sounded hopeful. That was Harold, Jack realized—the kid was always trying to believe things were okay.

But they weren't okay.

"I suppose," Frances told her little brother, but her tone was wary.

Alexander suddenly sprang up and started walking back and forth. "I know the Careys don't mean to be cruel. . . ."

"How do *you* know?" Jack suddenly shot back. "Look at how awful O'Reilly is. . . . Doesn't he do the Reverend's bidding? Haven't you noticed? What are you, st—"

Jack had to stop himself just then; he had almost

said *stupid*. But then he'd seen Alexander's face, and in a flash he remembered the pages that Eli had struggled to work on in that terrible schoolroom. Jack knew enough to realize it was the same way for Alexander.

"Of course I've noticed how O'Reilly is, Jack," Alexander said. He had stopped pacing.

Jack took a deep breath. "I'm sorry," he said. "Go on."

The older boy squared his shoulders and resumed pacing. "What I meant about the Careys is they haven't hurt us. But that's not enough. We shouldn't have to live this way, should we?"

"Live how?" Frances asked.

"I mean . . . ," Alexander began, but he couldn't seem to find the words. He looked to Jack. This time, Jack knew they were thinking alike.

"He means we shouldn't live in fear!" Jack said.

Alexander snapped his fingers. "Exactly! We can't go on worrying all the time about whether we're going to do something that'll get us punished or sent away. And the Reverend's supposed to believe in right and wrong, but what if he just believes in being right all the time?"

"But at least we're safe here!" Frances protested.

Jack could see the doubt in her face. "Safe for now," he pointed out. "Until Reverend Carey catches us talking to Eli. Or until he finds out about Wanderville. Do you think he and Mrs. Carey are going to approve of us coming out here on our own?"

Nobody said anything for a moment. Then Alexander spoke up.

"I . . . I guess I thought everything was going to be better once we built Wanderville again," he said. "I thought we'd all be back together. And then something would work out the way I planned."

He dropped back down on the grass and sighed. All Alexander wanted, Jack knew, was for Wanderville to be as real as possible.

Alexander straightened. "The only way we can all be together again and truly rebuild Wanderville is to leave the Careys'."

Jack grinned. For the first time in days, his friend sounded like he had back in Kansas. He looked over at Harold, who was nodding excitedly. Even Frances seemed to agree.

Then Alexander turned to him. "Right, Jack?"

"Right," Jack said. "But first we have to help Eli. We owe him. And"—Jack hesitated—"and we should help him because we *can*. Because . . ."

Frances cut in gently. "Because you're thinking of all the children we left behind on the ranch in Kansas, aren't you, Jack?" Her voice turned even softer. "The ones we couldn't save."

Jack looked down at his feet. Yes, he was thinking about the kids back at the Pratcherds'. His thinking about them was like the sound of the crickets this time of year. It was always there, slipping under his other thoughts, but then sometimes, like now, it was all around him.

"Yes," he said finally. "And all the other kids, on all the orphan trains. I mean . . . helping Eli is the least we can do."

"We'll do it," Alexander said. "We'll get Eli out."

And so the four of them began to devise a plan. They talked and planned until dusk fell and they had to head back to the barn. As they approached the fence, Jack grabbed one of the wild apples that grew at the edge of the clearing.

"Don't bother," Frances said. "The Careys said those apples won't be any good. They've been growing on their own for too long."

But Jack couldn't help it—the fruit looked ripe, and he was hungry. He took a bite, expecting the fruit to be bitter. But it wasn't. It was fine—pretty good, in fact. The Reverend wasn't right about everything.

The next day Frances wrote a note on the torn-out back flyleaf of her *Third Eclectic Reader*. Blank space in that book was becoming more and more precious, but this was important:

Dear House Kids,

The boy in the schoolroom is named Eli, and he is our friend.

He did nothing wrong. It's all a mistake, but the Rev. won't understand.

We're going to liberate Eli. Will you help us?

Write back yes or no. Then wait for instructions.

—Barn Kids

She tucked the note beneath a slat under the basket lid. Then she hid in the yard and waited.

She'd been crouching behind a tree for nearly half an hour before the door to the house opened and Sarah came out with the washtub. Frances nearly fell over with relief. Laundry was one of the few chores that brought Sarah and Anka out to the yard for any length of time, but Frances hadn't known for sure which day was wash day.

She rushed over to Sarah and held out the basket. "Mrs. Carey said to return this."

But Sarah just hurried past her toward the water pump. "I've got to fill the tub," she said. "You can just take it inside yourself."

Frances leaped ahead of her and stood in front of the pump. "Um . . . I'll set it down by the steps. And then *you* should take it inside." She looked Sarah right in the eye.

Sarah blinked, confused for a moment. But then she nodded. "Oh! Of course!" So Frances left the basket at the steps while Sarah filled the washtub.

Later that day, Mrs. Carey handed Frances the same basket at suppertime. Frances felt fluttery and anxious carrying it back over the fence to Wanderville, where Jack, Alexander, and Harold waited.

"Do you think they wrote back?" Jack asked as Frances began to pull food from the basket.

"I hope so," said Frances. "I said in the note to write back yes or no. And I know Sarah got the note, so . . ."

She went silent as she reached the bottom of

the basket. There was no note. She checked the lid. Nothing. She ran her fingers along the slats inside the basket, hoping that a piece of paper might be caught under one of them. But there wasn't.

Her heart sank. *They didn't send a message back.*

At least Harold was excited about the food. "Here's an apple!" he exclaimed. Only her little brother would still be excited about apples after days of working in an orchard, Frances thought.

But that wasn't what Harold was yelling about. "Look, Frances!" he cried, holding out the apple.

And there, carved neatly into the side, were the letters *Y-E-S*.

23
INSIDE THE HOUSE

The geese and chickens were making their daybreak noises, but Frances was already awake.

In fact, she was running—sprinting from the barn past the water pump, the chapel, and the yard—heading straight for the Careys' house in the gray dawn light. Her shoes were unbuttoned and her shirttails trailed behind her. She clambered up the stairs to the kitchen door and fell against it.

"Mrs. Carey!" she cried, half out of breath.

The door swung open. "My child, what's the matter?" the Reverend's wife whispered. Behind her were Eleanor and Olive, wide-eyed, their hair still unbraided.

"My brother," Frances gasped. "He has a fever. . . ." She turned and looked back at the barn.

Without another word, Mrs. Carey was out the door and hurrying toward the barn, with Frances running ahead to lead her. The Carey girls followed, too.

Harold was in his straw bale bed, his face flushed and wet with perspiration. "Frannie," he moaned. Alexander and Jack were crouched next to him, trying to give him some water from a tin cup.

"He wouldn't get out of bed this morning," Frances explained, her pulse racing anxiously. "And then I felt how hot his forehead was."

Mrs. Carey put her hand to Harold's head. "Oh, dear. The boy ought to be inside. Olive, help me carry him, and, Eleanor, gather his things." One of the Carey girls (the taller one, Frances noted) came over and helped her mother pick up Harold, who only whimpered as he was lifted out of bed. "Frances, he's your brother, so you'll come in with us, won't you?" Mrs. Carey asked.

"Oh, well . . . of course," Frances said slowly. "But first . . . I have to find his lucky pebble! He loves it, and—and he feels better when he can hold it in his hand! Right, Harold?" As she spoke, she began to search the corners of the barn.

"*Pebble*," Harold said weakly as he was being wrapped in a blanket. "Want . . . pebble . . ."

"You see?" Frances said. "He misplaced it, and I'm the only one here who knows what it looks like." Jack and Alexander nodded at that. "I'll bring it to him as soon as I find it!"

Mrs. Carey was becoming impatient. "He needs a cold compress, not a lucky charm. Come on, Olive."

They took Harold out of the barn while Frances and the boys watched. As he was being carried out, Harold caught Frances's eye and smiled just a little. In another few moments, he was inside the house.

"Whew!" Jack said, turning to Frances. "That was close. Good thing you thought up that business with the pebble."

Frances let out the breath she'd been holding. "That's for sure." She needed to stay outside for now; later she'd have a good excuse for getting into the house.

"Now we wait for the next step," said Alexander. "Let's hope Harold does his part."

Mrs. Carey smelled a little like oatmeal. Or maybe it was the house, Harold thought, which carried the scent of hot breakfast cooking. He wondered if there was a kind of fever that could be treated with bacon and if there was a way to convince Mrs. Carey that he had it. Because it sure was a bother pretending to be sick. He'd had to run all around the barn with his coat on in order to get his face hot enough to fool the Careys.

He'd kept his eyes squeezed shut the whole time he was being carried inside, but he finally opened them a peek after he'd been tucked in bed. He was in the upstairs room where the other children's beds were. Frances had hated that room, but truthfully it wasn't that bad. In fact, it was kind of nice. He shut his eyes again while Mrs. Carey put cool, wet cloths over his forehead. It wasn't long before he began to doze off, just like a real sick person, and he was awfully proud of his performance.

He woke to see four faces looking down at him. Faces that he knew but hadn't seen in days.

"Harold!" whispered George. "You're here!"

Behind George were Nicky, Sarah, and Anka.

Harold sat up and grinned. "We got your apple message," he told them as he reached into his pocket for the note that he'd brought. He handed it to Sarah, who unfolded it. It was a list of instructions that Frances and Jack had written out the night before.

Sarah and Nicky looked over the note. "'Get the key to the schoolroom,'" Sarah read aloud. She shook her head. "The Reverend and Mrs. Carey each have keys, but they keep their sets with them at all times."

"Is impossible," Anka added.

"But we can help with the other things on this list," Nicky said.

Harold nodded, but he felt a lump in his throat. The key to the schoolroom was the most important part! Without it, how were they going to get Eli out?

"You don't look so good," George said. "Are you sure you're not just a little bit sick, for real?"

"Yeah," Nicky said. "When you're sick, you get toast with butter and jam."

"Really?" Harold lay back on the pillows and hoped he still looked feverish. He wondered what kind of jam Mrs. Carey would put on his toast.

Meanwhile, the others began to make their beds and tidy the bedroom. Harold couldn't believe how neatly and cheerfully they worked. Back at the orphanage in New York, making beds was a dreaded task because it could never be done quite right and the matrons would always yell about the covers being lumpy. But here, even George knew how to make the corners tuck in perfectly. Nicky was humming a merry-sounding song as he swept the floor, and

Sarah and Anka shook pillows in rhythm to the tune. It looked almost fun. No, it *was* fun.

Harold wished Frances and Jack and Alexander could see what it was like in here. Maybe they wouldn't have to leave! They could all live together in the house and then go out to visit Wanderville. Of course, that depended on whether they would be allowed to play out there. Harold had a feeling the Careys wouldn't approve, which meant they'd have to sneak over. But then, they weren't supposed to lie—did sneaking count as lying?

Thinking about all this made Harold's head feel hot for real. It wasn't a good feeling, but at least maybe now he'd get extra jam on his toast.

By the afternoon Harold had consumed not only toast and jam, but some hot soup, a mug of tea that smelled like cinnamon, and a dish of applesauce. It was all delicious, but it was a little boring to sit there with Mrs. Carey watching him take every bite and slurp every spoonful.

Later, he was allowed to go downstairs and sit in the kitchen while the other children worked. Harold and Nicky peeled potatoes for supper while Anka and Sarah sliced cucumbers to make pickles. Before long, Nicky and George began to hum again, a song Harold didn't know.

"Let's sing the Rock Candy Mountain song!" Harold suggested. "With the part that Ned Handsome made up about Wanderville!"

Sarah wrinkled her nose. "You mean that old hobo song?"

George shrugged. "I don't remember how it goes."

So Harold started to sing:

In the Big Rock Candy Mountains, all the sheriffs are stone-blind,
And the children from Wanderville don't pay 'em any mind. . . .

But nobody was joining in, and Harold couldn't sing so well when he had to sing all by himself. He let the song trail off into a mumble.

"No more song about sheriff and orphan train," Anka said, frowning. "Hate to think of those things."

"We live here now," George said. "Not Wanderville."

"But—" Harold protested.

"We have new songs," Nicky said. "The Reverend taught us this one. . . ."

With banner and with badge we come,
An army true and strong,
To fight against the hosts of rum,
And this shall be our song.

Then Sarah and Anka and George joined in:

We love the clear cold water springs,
Supplied by gentle showers.
We feel the strength cold water brings.
The victory is ours.

If you asked Harold, the song wasn't as jolly as the hobo song. You had to sing it like you were marching, and from the way it plodded along, it was like marching in mud.

But he tried to learn the song, and two other songs that Nicky and the others had learned. They were all about how cold water was better than liquor, but *everyone* knew *that*, Harold thought. He'd never tasted liquor, of course, but he knew it smelled exactly like shoes on fire. Couldn't folks tell the difference between that stuff and cold water? Why did they need so many songs to explain? And as good as cold water was, it wasn't *nearly* as delicious as rock candy, especially not a Rock Candy Mountain.

That night, Harold lay in bed—*his* bed, Mrs. Carey had told him. His stomach was full and happy, but everything else felt funny. He kept looking around—like he was searching for something, but he didn't know what. He could see, out the window and in the moonlight, a glimpse of the barn where Frances and Jack and Alexander were working on the next part of their plan. That was good. But he couldn't shake the feeling that something was missing. Was it because Frances wasn't here? Or was it because of what he'd seen behind the shed, when that farmhand hit Mr. Pike again and again? Nobody in this house talked about Mr. Pike or Eli. Harold thought about Eli stuck all by himself in that schoolroom. Could he hear them making their beds and singing their songs?

Something on the bedroom windowsill caught his eye. He went over to pick it up. It was Anka's little wooden doll, the one she'd brought to the first Wanderville back in Kansas. It had stood in a special spot there, on a shelf in the trees that had made the place feel like a real house, only better. Harold knew that Anka had brought the doll with her when they'd left Kansas. He'd figured the next time he saw it, it would be in a place that felt like home.

But this wasn't home. He knew that now.

24
TO STEAL A KEY

Jack couldn't stop going over all the details in his head that night. According to the list they'd sent into the house with Harold, the first thing they needed was the key to the schoolroom. But, of course, it was up to the kids in the house to get it and unlock the door. He looked out across the yard to the lighted windows of the house. What if nobody could get the key? The whole plan depended on that part.

At least Jack and Frances and Alexander had the next few things on their list. The kids from the house had slipped them into the supper basket—a sheaf of writing paper, a pen, and ink. Now the three of them in the barn were working on the next part of the plan.

Or, really, it was Frances who was doing most

of the work. "My hand's getting numb!" she complained as she finished writing out another page. She was huddled over a makeshift desk that they'd made from a wooden crate, scribbling furiously by lantern light. "Why am I doing this again?"

"So we can put those pages in the schoolroom as a decoy and make it look like Eli completed his punishment," Alexander reminded her. "If we just unlocked the schoolroom and let him out, there'd be trouble."

"I know why *we're* doing it, silly," Frances grumbled, straightening the growing stack. "What I want to know is why *I* have to be the one to write all the pages! Is it because it's *my* little brother's fault that Eli's locked up?"

Jack laughed. "No! It's because you can write the best. And the fastest." He felt a little sorry for Frances, but she was filling the pages in no time—with the words to nursery rhymes, old songs, poems she must have known by heart from her *Third Eclectic Reader*. Of course, if Reverend Carey ever read the pages closely he'd know that they weren't the sermon he'd assigned Eli to write out fifty times. But Jack would make sure Eli was free before the Reverend even read the first word.

"I'm running out of things to write," Frances said with a sigh. "I've written out 'Mary Had a Little Lamb' six times in a row! *Now* what?"

"Just write whatever comes to mind," Jack suggested. "You've only got a couple of pages left to go!"

Frances nodded wearily and dipped her pen into the inkwell, then went back to writing.

Alexander had started pacing again, the way he always did when he talked about plans. "We'll sneak into the house tomorrow and get the pages to Eli. Then the next time the Reverend checks on him, he'll start to read the pages. That'll be Eli's chance to slip out."

"And then we'll shut the schoolroom door on the Reverend and lock it from the outside," Jack said.

Frances looked up from her writing and glared at him. Jack knew she didn't approve of this part of the plan—she thought it was mean.

"We'll lock it just for a minute or two, Frances, I promise," Jack said. "Just long enough to give Eli a chance to escape . . ."

"And just long enough to let Sarah and Nicky and Anka and George gather their things," Alexander said. "And then we'll all hit the road."

At breakfast the next day, Harold kept his eyes on the keys on Mrs. Carey's belt. Last night, he had seen her give them to one of her daughters (he still didn't know who was who), who in turn had taken a bowl of soup into the schoolroom for Eli. But then Olive or Eleanor gave the keys right back, and as far as he could tell, there was never a chance to just *take* the keys. What could he do?

The Reverend sipped his tea at the head of the table. "Children, one of you has taken a pen and ink from my study," he announced. "Some paper, too. For what purpose do you need these things?"

Harold tried not to look over at Sarah too quickly. She had taken the writing things last night and packed them in the supper basket to send out to the barn kids. She turned a little pale but remained silent. So did the other kids. *They don't want to lie*, he realized.

But then George spoke up. "I borrowed them, sir. I was teaching Harold the Cold Water Army song, and I wanted to write down the words. Right, Harold?"

"Right." Harold nodded.

"Very well," said Reverend Carey, giving both boys a stern look. "But you must ask before you borrow something." He stood up and excused himself from the table, and a moment or two later, Harold heard him close the door to his study.

"Thanks," Harold whispered to George. He was both glad that George was still his friend and sorry that he had to lie for his sake—just as Eli had.

As the children cleared the dishes from the breakfast table, Harold noticed one of the Carey girls—Eleanor, he thought—placing a bowl of oatmeal on a tray. *For Eli*, Harold realized. He hung back and watched Eleanor get the key from Mrs. Carey and walk down the hall toward the schoolroom. Then he followed her with his quietest footsteps.

He watched her unlock the door with the key and go inside. The door was wide open, he realized—could he slip into the schoolroom without her noticing? His legs felt shaky as he took the first steps. But then he pretended he was a ghost floating and invisible as he tucked himself behind the open door. It worked! Eleanor hadn't seen him.

"You're sure taking a long time to finish your punishment, aren't you?" she said to Eli.

"Yes, ma'am" was all Eli said in reply.

Eleanor must not have liked being called *ma'am*,

because she muttered "Suit yourself" and set the bowl down hard.

Harold watched from behind the door as she walked out. He did it! He had gotten into the school-room and he hadn't even had to steal the key! Now all he had to do was—

The door shut at that moment with a loud *thud*. And then Harold heard the key turning in the lock. Locking it.

Uh-oh. Harold had been so excited about sneaking into the schoolroom that he had forgotten how the door worked. Now *he* was locked inside, just like Eli.

Eli looked over from his desk and gave a wry half smile. "Are you being punished, too, Red?"

25
THE FAKE FIGHT AND THE REAL FIGHT

The house kids were supposed to send a message letting the barn kids know they'd gotten the schoolroom key, but there hadn't been a word all morning.

Frances was getting nervous. She'd wrapped the decoy pages in her shawl, which she then tied around her waist. Now she was working in the garden, waiting for the next part of the plan to begin. She kept looking over at the schoolroom window, though she knew it wasn't likely she'd see anything—Jack had said it was too high up in the room to give a good view from either side.

As far as their plan was concerned, though, the most important window was the one in the kitchen. Jack and Alexander were at the woodpile by the barn making sure they remained in sight of the house. At the right moment, the two of them would stage a fistfight, and if all went well, the Careys would spot them from the kitchen and run out to break up the ruckus. Then, in the meantime, Frances would sneak into the house with the decoy pages.

But nothing would happen until they had the schoolroom key. Frances began to chew her lip with worry. She knew it would look suspicious to be working in the same spot in the garden for too long, and she began to glance around, wondering if anyone noticed her. She saw Olive and Eleanor out for a stroll, so she crouched down and started weeding, hoping to avoid them.

"Frances!"

She jumped at the sound of her name. *Pipe down, Harold!* she thought.

Then she straightened up. *Harold?* He was supposed to be in the house! She looked all around and then heard him again.

"Frannie! I'm locked inside!"

He *was* in the house—he was calling from the schoolroom window! She could see his shock of red hair in the narrow space, and his hand reaching out, waving frantically. He must have climbed up to reach the window—not a surprise, since Frances knew Harold could scale trees like a squirrel.

She rushed over below the window. "What happened? Are you being punished? What did you *do*?"

"I didn't do anything! Eleanor locked me in!"

"What?" cried a voice from behind Frances. It was one of the Carey girls. "I did not lock you in!" Eleanor called up to Harold. "It must have been Olive!"

"I did no such thing!" Olive protested, her face turning bright red. "Not on purpose, I mean!"

The Carey girls were confused. Frances, though, had figured it out—Harold must have sneaked into the schoolroom, and Olive had locked the door. It had been accidental, of course—whoever had made the mistake (Olive, perhaps), Frances could see that both girls were flustered and felt bad about it. But then that gave her an idea. . . .

She turned to face the Carey girls. "You locked my *little brother* up?" she cried in a horrified voice. "My little brother, who's *sick*?"

"N-not me," Eleanor sputtered. "At least, I don't think so. . . ."

"One of you did," said Frances, her eyes narrowing. "Or maybe both of you. My poor, sick brother, what did he ever do to you?"

Up at the window, Harold began to cough loudly.

"It was an accident," Olive said. "No need for Mother to know, right?" She glanced over at Eleanor, who nodded nervously.

"Of *course* not," said Frances. "We can just go in quietly and let him out. I won't say a word, and I'll make Harold promise, too."

Olive blew out a breath of relief. "Good. We'll just need an excuse to get the keys from Mother."

Frances smiled. "I'm sure we can figure something out."

"Did you hear something?" Jack asked Alexander as they waited over by the woodpile.

"No, why?" Alexander asked.

"I thought I heard someone yelling," Jack said, motioning to Alexander to stay quiet. The two waited for several moments, and Jack listened for the voice again. He didn't want to say anything, but he could've sworn it was Harold, calling his sister's name.

But there was nothing more. Finally Jack shrugged. "Never mind."

They went back to stacking wood and discussing the best ways to stage their fake fight.

"You should shove me first," Alexander suggested.

"Then I'll roll up my sleeves and take a swing, but you'll duck so that I'll miss."

Jack wasn't so sure. "What if you don't miss? And why do I have to be the one to start it?"

"Because you're the hotheaded one," Alexander said with a grin.

"What? No, I'm not!"

"Sure you are. It's why I have to be the one in charge."

Jack snorted at that. "Oh, really?" Now Alexander was pulling that I'm-the-leader stuff again. "Well, if you're so smart, and I'm the one with the temper, why are you trying to provoke me now, before we've even gotten the signal?"

He was trying to be logical, but he could feel his own face getting warm. Why did Alexander have to be such a pain sometimes? They'd been getting along better for the past few days, but that all had suddenly changed.

"Don't be a turkey," Alexander shot back. "I'm not trying to—wait a second . . . what's going on?" He peered over Jack's shoulder at the house.

Jack turned and saw Frances being led through the back door of the house by the Carey girls.

Why is she going inside? Jack wondered. He couldn't see the expressions on any of the three girls' faces from here, but it seemed as if Olive and Eleanor sure were keeping an eye on Frances. "I don't understand," he told Alexander. "She was supposed to wait for us to fight!"

"Then let's fight now!" Alexander said. "What are we delaying for?"

Jack would have loved nothing more than to shove Alexander just then, for real. But something was wrong inside that house. He knew it.

"What if she's in trouble?" Jack wondered. By now his mind was racing: Maybe Olive and Eleanor had caught Frances with the key and were taking her to Reverend Carey. Or maybe they had brought her inside because Harold had gotten hurt. It was all starting to add up, in dozens of awful ways. "That shouting I heard . . . I think it was Harold!"

Alexander's eyes widened. "Are you sure?"

"I think so," said Jack. "I really think something's wrong in there. We should sneak inside and help."

For just a moment, Alexander seemed to agree. But then he straightened his shoulders and looked down at Jack as if he were three feet taller, instead of just of a couple of inches. "No," he said firmly. "We'll do what we planned with the fight. Create a distraction out here instead."

Jack looked back toward the house. His hands were clenched into nervous fists. *He's wrong*, he thought. *I know he's wrong.*

"Come on," Alexander said, taking a step toward Jack, as if daring him. "Or are you chicken? That's why you're second fiddle around here."

Jack took a deep breath and shoved Alexander. Hard. So hard, in fact, that the older boy staggered backward and fell.

"What?" he yelped. "You pig! I'll slug you for real!"

But Jack wasn't listening. He was already running toward the house.

26
BEHIND LOCKED DOORS

Olive, Frances realized, was the shorter one of the sisters, and the cleverer one, too. She'd gotten the keys from Mrs. Carey with no trouble at all. "We need to unlock the cellar and bring up a few more pickle crocks," she'd told her mother.

"Good idea," Mrs. Carey had said. She'd hardly looked up from her work on the sewing machine as she handed the key ring over.

Then Frances and Eleanor followed Olive into the pantry and watched as she unlocked a trapdoor in the corner of the pantry floor.

Olive spoke under her breath to Frances. "That way it's not a lie," she said.

The girls left the cellar door open and ducked down the hall to the schoolroom. "I'll keep watch here and make sure Mother's not coming," Eleanor whispered, while Olive stood ready with the key.

"Go in and fetch your brother," she told Frances as she unlocked the door. "Make sure he keeps quiet about this. And keep an eye on him from now on, would you?"

"Sure." Frances patted her shawl where the pages were hidden. She'd hand them off to Eli and tell him to wait for the Reverend to come in. Then she'd get Harold and slip out. "Don't worry."

Olive pushed open the door and let Frances go inside.

"Eli?" she whispered. "Harold?" The rows of desks were curiously empty.

"Frances!" Harold called. He was up on the sill of the high window.

"Shh! Why are you still up there?" Frances said, trying to contain her panic. "You're going to break your neck!"

"It's easier to get up than to get down," Harold said.

"Never mind! Where's Eli?" Frances hurriedly pulled out the sheaf of papers and dropped them onto one of the desks.

"He was standing over there behind the door a

moment ago." Harold motioned to the spot where Frances had just entered. "But now he's gone."

Frances whirled around. Eli had slipped out through the open door!

She ran into the hall. There was no Eli, only Olive and Eleanor standing there wide-eyed.

"Did you let that boy out?" she asked them.

"Olive did," said Eleanor.

"I did *not*!" said Olive. "He just ran out! He went that way!" She pointed in the direction of the kitchen.

Frances was sure he'd escaped out the back door of the house. But before she could say anything, they heard footsteps clomping down the hall toward them.

Eleanor gasped and lunged at the open door to the schoolroom, pulling it shut. Olive hurriedly locked it and hid the keys behind her back. *Harold's still in there!* Frances realized with horror, but the footsteps were coming closer, and there was nothing she could do.

The footsteps were Jeb's. He stopped and looked at his sisters and Frances suspiciously. "What in the blazes just happened?" he said. "I thought I saw that darky boy run out through here!"

"Don't call him that!" Frances said. "His name is Eli."

"And . . . and . . . we don't know what you're talking about, Jeb!" said Eleanor, folding her arms nervously in front of her.

Frances could tell she wasn't a very good liar, probably because she'd had to keep a promise to the Reverend all these years. "She means that Eli is still in the schoolroom," Frances told Jeb, thinking quickly. "See, I'll show you!" She knocked on the schoolroom door. *"Eli, you're in there, right?"* she called. *"Knock if you're in there!"* If Harold could knock in reply, Jeb would think it was Eli.

There was only silence. The three Carey teenagers gathered around Frances, and together they stared at the door. Frances felt her chest pounding. What if Harold couldn't climb down from the windowsill?

Tap-tap! came the sound at last from the other side of the door.

Frances nearly fell over with relief. "See?" she told Jeb.

"Yes, *see*?" Olive said. Though, like Eleanor, she crossed her arms anxiously.

Just then, there were more footsteps, and Mrs.

Carey appeared in the hall. "Olive!" she said sternly. "You left the cellar door open! Go and lock it, will you? And then return the keys to me."

Olive mumbled a quick "Yes, Mother" and hurried down the hall.

Then Mrs. Carey turned to Frances. "Why, Frances! Are you here to see Harold?"

With her still-pounding heart, Frances could only nod for a moment. How many lies was she going to have to tell today? It felt as if her brain were doing somersaults.

"I've got his lucky pebble," she said. "Eleanor said he's upstairs . . . uh, right?"

She held her breath and hoped Mrs. Carey wouldn't look around the house for Harold. She could tell by the expression on Eleanor's face that she thought the same thing.

"I suppose he is," said Mrs. Carey. "You may go up and say hello."

"Thank you!" Frances gasped as she darted up the stairs. She had never been so relieved to get away.

To Jack's surprise the back door to the house opened as he approached the steps. Nicky let him in, with his finger to his lips to indicate that Jack should keep quiet.

"What's going on?" Nicky whispered. "We just saw you shove Alexander!" Behind him were Sarah and Anka and George—they'd been peeling potatoes and must have observed him and Alexander fighting through the window. Jack peered out back at the woodpile, but Alexander was gone.

"Never mind that," Jack whispered back. "Where's Harold? Is Frances all right?"

Sarah shrugged. "Harold's upstairs in bed. And Frances just came through here with Eleanor and Olive. I've no idea why. They wouldn't tell us."

Jack nodded. He was just as confused as they were.

George pointed to the other end of the big kitchen. "You can't see it from here, but there's a pantry. They went in there to get something!"

Jack went over to the pantry doorway. No one was in there, but Jack stood inside a moment to marvel at all the casks and bins and sacks of provisions, the jars of jelly and preserves all lined up on the shelves. . . .

"Someone's coming!" Nicky hissed. "You have to hide!"

Jack spotted the open trapdoor in the corner of the pantry—he could see there were stairs leading down to a cellar. He tiptoed across the first few steps, then crouched and leaped down into the cellar like a cat to make the least amount of noise possible.

He ducked out of sight of the trapdoor as he heard footsteps on the floor overhead. Hardly daring to breathe, he waited. Jack looked around—one small window let in scant daylight, and though his eyes had yet to adjust to the dimness, he could make out bins of apples and potatoes.

Then, suddenly, the cellar darkened further as the trapdoor closed above him. Jack heard a key clink in a lock.

It was at the very same moment that Jack realized he wasn't alone. He could hear someone breathing.

"Hello?" he whispered.

Jack had barely spoken the words before something came at him in a pale flash and hit him in the head with a *thunk*!

27
DOWN IN THE CELLAR

"An onion," Jack said, rubbing the side of his head. "You threw an *onion* at me?"

"Sorry!" Eli said. "I didn't know it was you! I was sure someone was coming to thrash me for escaping."

"It's all right. Glad it was a small onion," Jack said as he looked down at the vegetable at his feet. "And it's better than throwing a hot potato."

Eli gave him a funny look. "Who was throwing hot potatoes around?"

Jack grinned. "Long story."

"Well, you might have time to tell me. We're locked in down here!"

Jack glanced around. "What about that window over there?" But as he looked, he could see it had only one tiny pane of glass that angled forward just enough to let air in.

"It doesn't open wide enough," Eli said.

"There's got to be another way out. Another exit, right?"

Eli sighed. "Yes, but . . . here, I'll show you." He led Jack to one end of the cellar where a few stone steps led up to a pair of tilted doors. Jack realized he'd seen these doors from the outside—they leaned against the side of the house below the kitchen window.

Eli pushed against the doors, but they didn't open. "See, they've got a board nailed across them to keep 'em shut. In fact, my old man had the job to hammer them down two summers ago."

"Maybe the nails are looser now," Jack suggested. "We could push together."

"Good idea." Eli leaned hard against the doors, and Jack joined him.

The wood creaked and groaned as they struggled, and they could feel the doors straining against the board on the other side.

"C'mon!" said Eli. They pushed again until the wood began to pop and splinter.

But no matter how many times they heaved, they

couldn't get the doors to move any further. Jack wondered how many pushes it would take to work the nails loose. He turned around and leaned back against the doors so that he could brace his feet and shove with his own weight. Eli did the same.

"Grrrr!" Jack grunted.

But the doors didn't open. Both boys stumbled down the stone steps and wiped their foreheads. *It's no use*, Jack thought.

But the noise of splintering wood continued. "What's that?" Eli asked.

Suddenly, Jack realized the sound was coming from the other side of the door. Someone outside was prying off the board! They could hear the squeak of nails being pulled out.

Eli looked at Jack, bewildered. "Who . . . who's out there?"

"I think it's—"

The board popped loose with a loud *snap*, and then the doors flew open.

"Alexander!"

Jack couldn't have been happier that he'd guessed right. The older boy waved his hatchet and grinned.

"Are we ever glad to see you!" Eli said.

"We sure are," Jack said, and he meant it.

"Figured you could use a little help with that door," he said to Jack. "You can shove hard, but sometimes it takes a lot more than that to break something."

Jack smiled. He knew Alexander was talking about more than doors.

Frances had gone upstairs "to visit Harold"—but of course there was only the empty room where the children slept. She'd sat on one of the beds for a few moments trying to calm down from all that had just happened down in the hallway.

But she knew she couldn't stay there long, so she'd crept back down the stairs. There were voices coming from the kitchen, so she headed toward the front door instead—if she could just find Jack and Alexander, maybe they could all work out a way to get Harold free. And then they could figure out where Eli was, too. . . .

She turned to cut through the parlor and almost collided with Reverend Carey. Frances gasped as she stopped short.

"I'm—I'm sorry," she stammered, her chest pounding all over again. She hadn't seen the Reverend since the incident behind the shed. She stared at the lapels of his black vest and remembered the blood on his shirt. A swell of helpless rage filled her head and she didn't dare look him in the face.

"What brings you here, my child?" he asked. "Oh—you must be visiting your sick young brother. But you look upset. Is the boy all right?"

"He's fine," Frances managed. But her eyes felt hot with the angry tears that she was trying to blink back. She remembered how kind he'd been at the train depot, and how nice his voice was when he played the fiddle at the prayer sessions. But now she couldn't see him like that. She never would again.

"But I see something else is wrong, Frances," Reverend Carey said gently. "What is it?"

Frances didn't want to answer—was that like lying? Yes, she knew, it *was* lying. And even though she hadn't made the promise not to lie like the other kids did, she realized that this was one time where she had no choice but to tell the truth.

"The other night we saw you," Frances said. "We saw what you did to Moses Pike."

The Reverend's face went pale. "My child," he whispered. "You should not have witnessed that. You don't understand. . . ."

"Yes, I do!" she cried. "There are people you want to help, but there are people you *don't* want to help, either. And you only want to help people when they live by your rules!"

Reverend Carey stepped back, shaking his head, unable to speak. His face had gone from pale to red, and Frances couldn't tell if it was from mortification or fury. She didn't want to find out.

She pushed past him and flew out the door.

"I sure am grateful that you got me out of that house," Eli told Jack and Alexander.

Jack nodded. "It's a good thing Alexander stayed outside."

"And that you went inside," Alexander said with a grin.

The boys had brought Eli to Wanderville while they tried to figure out what to do next. Eli had told them about how he'd slipped out of the schoolroom but that he didn't know what had happened to Harold.

"Let's hope Frances figured out a way to get him out," Alexander said. "We should go back over to the house."

"Not me," Eli said. "I ain't going anywhere near that house and that lowdown preacher again. Not now, not ever. I'm staying right here in Wanderville."

"But what about your pa?" Jack said.

"I'm not living with him, either. He doesn't want me around anyway."

"Well . . ." Alexander exchanged a look with Jack. "Of course you're welcome in Wanderville. The thing is, Wanderville isn't just this spot here behind the fence. At least, not for us. It's anywhere we go."

"And *we're* planning on leaving the farm," Jack continued. "Us and Harold and Frances and the kids in the house. As soon as possible."

Eli didn't say anything for a moment.

"So that means . . . ," he said hesitantly.

"You're coming with us," Jack finished.

Eli's face burst into a huge smile. "Right," he said.

Alexander reached over and shook his hand. "Congratulations. You're our newest citizen!"

Eli laughed and shook Jack's hand, too. Then he looked around. "I just need to get a few things from my pop's place while he's still out in the fields." He ran over and climbed the split-rail fence.

"Eli, wait . . . ," Jack called, remembering the

last time he'd seen Mr. Pike. "What if he's not out in . . ."

But Eli was already gone.

Jack turned toward the fence to run after him, but Alexander clapped him on the shoulder. "Just give Eli a minute, and then go and make sure he's all right. And I'll go by the house and see if I can find Frances."

"Here!" gasped a familiar voice from behind them. "I'm here!" called Frances. "I finally found you two!" She stopped by the fence to catch her breath. "I ran everywhere looking."

"Where's Harold?" Jack asked. "Is he still locked up?"

"That's why I was trying to find you! So I could tell you—"

"Wait," Alexander interrupted. "There's Harold right now."

He was pointing over to the back of the barn, and Jack turned to look. Sure enough, there was Harold, his eyes wide.

Mrs. Carey stood behind him with a firm grasp on his shirt collar. Beside her was Reverend Carey, his face stern as he stared across at Jack and his friends.

"Come here at once," he ordered.

28
WORDS NOT SPOKEN

If it hadn't been for Harold, she would have just run off. It was all Frances could do to keep from dragging her feet as the three of them made their way over to where the Careys stood with Harold. The Reverend grasped something in his hand, a white stick of some kind. A ruler? She cringed to think of the punishment.

Harold had his *I'm sorry* look on his face. Frances could only nod and try to hide her own fear and dread.

But when she finally stood in front of Reverend Carey, she saw that the thing in his hand wasn't a stick at all, but a rolled sheaf of paper. Some of the pages came loose as he held the sheaf out for the children to see.

Frances recognized them. They were the pages that she had written and placed in the schoolroom.

"Who wrote these?" the Reverend asked. "I'm well aware it wasn't Eli."

"We were just trying to help him," Jack said.

"I know what you were doing," Reverend Carey said. "But I want to know, *who wrote them?*"

Frances stepped forward. "I did," she whispered. She was getting that squeezed-too-tight feeling, and she couldn't bring herself to look up.

The Reverend held one of the scribbled pages right in front of her face. "And these words," he asked, his voice a little less sharp. "They are your . . . thoughts?"

Frances stared at her own cursive handwriting and remembered. *Write whatever comes to mind,* Jack had said. And there, on the page, was just that, in crazed half sentences:

One day soon we'll be gone and we'll go to California—we'll be free—California—find gold! Hope we can escape—Not Eli's fault he missed so much school. His pa's a drunkard! Not fair, not fair at all—have to escape what if Miss DeHaven comes back—makes us work in

a factory—or go back to the orphanages don't
want to—wish there was a train, an anywhere
train—in the big rock candy mountains all
the chores are fun as pie and all of us in
Wanderville are free forever nigh—

Frances's face burned as she read the words she'd scribbled. She'd written pages like this—about her old life on the streets, the orphan train ride, all the things she'd seen. She'd written about how she wished they could go back to Kansas and save all the kids at the Pratcherds', then find treasure and live someplace where nobody would force them to work or send them away from their brothers and sisters. . . .

She took a quavering breath. She hadn't thought anyone was going to read what she'd written.

Mrs. Carey spoke up. "These words are how you feel, Frances?"

Frances wiped a tear from her face. Funny how she'd never made that promise to the Careys about not lying. Now she couldn't lie to them even when she wanted to.

"Yes, ma'am," she said. "And it's how the rest of us feel, too. We want to be on our own."

From behind her she could sense the boys

nodding, and she heard Alexander say, "That's right, ma'am."

The Reverend and Mrs. Carey exchanged a solemn look that Frances couldn't decipher. Then Mrs. Carey let go of Harold's collar to draw out another piece of paper from the sheaf her husband held. "There is this page as well," she said.

Right away Frances recognized her little brother's handiwork. Harold must have drawn the picture while he was locked in the schoolroom—taking advantage of the paper and pencils that were available there. He'd drawn the wild apple trees and the split-rail fence and the old stone chimney; he'd also put in the creek and the pine trees and the courthouse log from the ravine in Kansas. He'd drawn himself swinging on a rope swing, with legs like stovepipes and a blocky body. And all around were smiling figures that Frances knew to be Alexander and Jack and George and Nicky and Anka and Sarah and another figure that she guessed was Eli.

Harold had come over and now he was pointing proudly. "That's you," he told Frances. And there she was in the drawing—she knew it was her because she was holding her book, the *Third Eclectic Reader*, with the broken spine.

At the top Harold had written: WANDRVILLE.

"What is this place?" Mrs. Carey asked the children. "You wrote this name, too, Frances—is it the place where you go play in the evenings?"

Jack spoke up. "It's the place that goes wherever we go. So we can call it home."

"And we might as well tell you," Alexander said, his voice shaky. "We think it's time we go somewhere else. We've caused so much trouble, after all. . . ."

Frances dared to look up at the Reverend. There was a stormy look on his face. He straightened up as if he were about to deliver a sermon. But then he bowed his head. "My children," he said, "it was our hope that this would be your home. But . . . I understand that there are different paths one can take in life."

Mrs. Carey was nodding at that.

"I have tried to cultivate all the trees in this orchard," he continued. "But even I have to admit there are some that grow best when they grow wild, and perhaps it's the same way with you children."

He looked straight at Frances suddenly. "And I've been wrong, too. I always thought I was helping everyone I could. But there have been those whose troubles I've ignored. Many years ago, the people who toiled on this farm were given their freedom, but I've been blind to the other things that have kept some of them from being truly free. I see now, and I will do my best to change that."

Frances knew he was talking about Eli's father. *Thank you*, she mouthed.

Jack spoke up. "If Miss DeHaven ever comes back, will you promise not to tell her where we went?"

"Yes," said the Reverend. "We can promise that."

Mrs. Carey was dabbing her eyes with a handkerchief. "This is not easy, letting you children go," she said. "But I know the sadness a house can have when a child is not happy there."

Reverend Carey gave a weary sigh. "Our oldest, Matthew."

Frances remembered hearing that he had become a missionary. She knew the Careys were proud of him, but it must have been hard for them knowing that he *wanted* to go so far away from home.

"Now perhaps you understand why we wanted to take you in," Mrs. Carey said. "And why we're letting you go. We just want all children to be happy."

Harold pointed to his drawing. "You can keep this," he told Mrs. Carey. "It shows us happy."

29
GOODBYE AND GOOD NIGHT

J ack was in the barn rolling up the few clothes
he wasn't wearing—his coat, extra socks, and a
hand-me-down shirt the Careys had given him—into
his sleeping blanket. He stuffed the roll into a feed
sack, his mind buzzing with excitement. He couldn't
believe they were free to leave!

"Packing already?" Alexander laughed. "We still
have to round everyone up to meet our newest citizen. Speaking of which, is Eli back?"

"Eli!" Jack said suddenly. "We forgot to check on
him!" It must have been an hour since Eli had gone
back to his father's shanty to get his things. Was he
all right?

Jack tossed down the feed sack and ran out of
the barn. He was relieved to see Eli coming up the

path carrying a bundle much like the one Jack had just packed.

"I'm ready," Eli said, swinging the bag over his shoulder.

"What about your pa? Did you see him?" Jack asked.

Eli scowled. "He just sat there in his rocker while I got my things. Said he figured I was going to run off and it was good riddance. Well, good riddance to him, too."

Jack looked at Eli's bundle. "It took you that long to pack *that*?"

"Well," Eli said, "actually, I went over to Clement's place and then Ora's to tell 'em goodbye. And . . . I asked them to look in on my pop once in a while. Make sure he gets a decent supper. . ." He looked down and shrugged. "My mama would have wanted me to do that."

Jack understood. He wondered if back in New York his mother was still taking care of his father when he came in late at night after visiting the taverns. Or was the bottle his only friend now?

The two boys continued down the path to the barn, stopping by the water pump to grab a drink. "Alexander says we'll set out at dawn tomorrow and follow the train tracks," Jack told Eli as Eli worked the pump. "Then we'll find a place to camp . . ."

Suddenly Eli stopped, his hand frozen on the pump handle, looking behind Jack.

Mr. Pike was walking slowly toward them. Jack wondered briefly if he was drunk, but when Jack looked up at his face, the man's eyes were clear and sober.

"Where are you going, Pop?" Eli asked quietly.

"The chapel," said Mr. Pike. "Gonna wait for the Reverend. He came by after you left. Said he was sorry about things. Said he'd pray with me if I wanted . . . if I wanted to stop."

Eli looked down. "Ain't the first time you promised that."

"I know," said Mr. Pike. "But since you're setting out to find yourself a better life, well . . . maybe I can find one, too. Maybe one day you'll come back and see if I did."

"Maybe I will," Eli said, his voice almost a whisper.

"Best to do it that way, instead of me letting you down all the time." Mr. Pike held out his hand, which trembled slightly.

Eli reached out and squeezed it.

Then Mr. Pike nodded goodbye and walked on to the chapel.

Frances was helping Harold collect all his things in the barn. It turned out he really *did* have a lucky pebble. And a lucky stick, leaf, horseshoe nail, and dead beetle.

"I'll keep them in my pocket," Harold insisted.

"Well, I suppose we need all the luck we can get," Frances said. Just then she looked up. "Sarah! Anka!"

The girls were standing in the barn doorway, Nicky and George just behind them. They were all holding bundles and baskets, and Sarah wore a shy smile. They came into the barn, followed by Eli and Jack, who grinned in surprise.

Alexander, who had been in the haymow, swung down on the ladder. "You're all here!" he exclaimed. "And you're all packed!"

Frances looked over in time to see Anka's awkward expression. Sarah exchanged glances with Nicky before speaking.

"Actually, we're here to bring supper," she said, holding up the basket. "And, well, to tell you something."

Frances already knew what Sarah was going to say, and she could tell, by the expression on Jack's face, that he did, too. She'd had a feeling deep down for days now, and then today, when she'd gone upstairs in the house and seen Anka's little wooden doll on the windowsill, she knew for sure.

It was Nicky who said it.

"Sarah and Anka and George and me," he began, "we like it here at the Careys'."

"So . . . we're staying," Sarah added.

Frances looked over at Alexander, who was scratching his head.

"You're not coming with us?" he said. "What about our town? What about Wanderville?"

"It's about home," Anka said softly. "We think this will be our home now."

Alexander didn't say anything for a minute. Then he sat down on one of the crates that they used as chairs in the barn. "I wanted us to stay together," he said, staring at the ground.

Jack went over and pulled up a crate. So did Frances. "You know how the Careys let us go because they knew we'd be happier someplace else?" Jack asked Alexander.

"It's the same thing," Frances added.

"I guess you're right," Alexander said. His voice was sad, but he still managed a half smile.

"And they'll be safe here," Jack pointed out. "Thanks to you."

Frances watched Alexander's face brighten a little more.

"I'm glad you and Harold and Jack are still coming with us," he said.

"Always," Frances told him.

She looked over at Harold, who, along with Nicky, was helping Sarah and Anka open the supper baskets.

"I have an idea," she said. "Let's have supper in Wanderville!"

All eight of them, along with Eli, had one last picnic together in the grass and the crumbled walls of the old house. Then they played and talked until the sky turned deep pink.

"I wish you would stay," Sarah told Frances as they finished their sandwiches. "I think you'd really like Eleanor and Olive."

"They're all right," Frances said. "But I want to see California. I'm going to miss you and Anka, though."

She leaned back in the grass and listened to the other conversations. Eli and Jack were talking about trains. Nicky was promising Alexander that he and the other house kids would come out and play in this Wanderville sometimes.

"Mrs. Carey says I have to be careful not to break my glasses," George was telling Harold. "So I can't go back to being a hobo."

"I'll send you a postcard," Harold said. "And we can trade good-luck tokens. Want my beetle?"

Finally, it was time for the four who were staying with the Careys to go inside for the night. There were hugs goodbye and promises to write. Sarah gave Frances two pencils and extra writing paper so she wouldn't have to keep tearing pages out of her *Third Eclectic Reader*.

Meanwhile, Anka showed Alexander the basket where she'd packed extra sandwiches for their journey, and Nicky handed Jack and Eli sacks full of provisions he'd managed to scrounge up for them.

"And when the Careys ask me where those potatoes went," he said, "I'll tell 'em the truth and take my lumps."

They all laughed.

"Thank you for everything," Frances called one

last time as Anka, Sarah, Nicky, and George climbed over the fence at dusk.

Then the five of them spread out their blankets to go to sleep. They all lay back and bade each other good-night by their hobo names:

"Night, Pennsylvania Kid."

"Good night, Gizzard."

"Sleep tight, Little Tomato Can."

"Good night, Swindler Jack."

Jack sat up and turned to Eli. "Wait, you need a hobo name!"

Frances watched as Eli sat up and scratched his head. Finally, he said, "Call me Bulldog."

They all agreed it was an excellent name.

After that, they lay back again, looking up at the deepening blue sky.

"It's the first time we've spent the night in the Missouri Wanderville," Frances mused.

"And also the last, since we're leaving tomorrow," Jack pointed out.

"It doesn't matter," Alexander said. "We're back under the stars."

30
THE FINAL ESCAPE

It was dawn when something nudged Jack in the side. Hard.

It shoved up against his ribs—it was a foot, Jack realized—a *boot*. Someone was trying to roll him over like a log. Jack squirmed onto his back and looked up to see the man standing over him: O'Reilly, with his stubbly red face.

"Just what are you up to?" he growled at Jack.

"What—what do you mean?" Jack managed to straighten up and get out from under that awful boot. The other children were just waking up, and he could hear Harold whimper at the sight of O'Reilly. Eli, Jack noticed, was already sitting up and glaring at the man.

"You little brats were supposed to be gone already.

But *this* one"—O'Reilly nodded toward Eli—"he ain't going nowhere. He stays here." He grabbed the boy's wrist. "*This* one's got to work for me, since his daddy's no good for the fields."

Alexander scrambled to his feet. "No! Eli's with us! And Reverend Carey said we could go."

O'Reilly smirked. "Yes, he said *you* could go. Reverend sent me out here to make sure you maggots weren't sneaking off with a—*arrrgh!*"

He left off with a sharp yowl as Eli pinched his forearm hard.

The boy wrenched himself free and dodged behind Jack. "Front gate," he gasped before he took off running. Then O'Reilly shoved past Jack and lit out after Eli in swift pursuit. After a moment they'd disappeared around the side of the barn.

"Oh, no," Harold whispered, while Frances stood, stunned.

"Get your things!" Alexander said, turning to grab one of the feed sack pouches they'd packed. "Eli's bag, too. Right, Jack?"

Jack just nodded, so anxious he could barely breathe.

A few moments later, the four of them crept along the fence at the edge of the farm, doing their best to stay out of sight of the house. But as they got closer to the front yard and the road beyond it, Jack could see, in the early-morning dimness, a light in one of the upstairs windows of the house. The light shifted as someone moved in the window. From the silhouette Jack thought it might be Mrs. Carey, but he couldn't be sure, and he didn't know why she'd be watching.

They were getting close to the front gate now. Did Eli mean to meet them there? *Or*, Jack thought, *at least try?*

But there was nobody there. Frances turned to Jack with panicked eyes. "What now?" she whispered, looking to him and Alexander. "Do we wait for Eli? Do we run for it?"

"Run for it!" Harold said, not whispering. "Look!"

Jack had been so preoccupied with searching for Eli at the front fence he hadn't thought to look beyond it, out in the road. But there, waiting at a small bend past the fence, was a wagon, a single-hitch with a horse that looked too scraggly to belong to the Careys. Clement Bay held the reins, and he nodded in their direction.

The four of them hesitated. Jack looked back to

see if Eli was coming. Frances grabbed his shoulder. "There!" she gasped. "There he is."

Jack turned just in time to see Eli stand in the bed of the wagon. He was grinning, but he waved frantically, as if to say, *hurry!*

Jack almost laughed out loud as they all ran the last few yards and climbed into the wagon bed. Frances got in first, then she and Alexander helped lift in Harold, and Jack swung up last.

"I outran O'Reilly," Eli bragged as the wagon began to move. "He's chased me before, but sooner or later he always stops when his knee goes funny. So I just took a chance and kept running. And then the fact that Clement was heading to town was just good luck."

"All I'm doing is headin' to the mercantile," Clement called from the front of the wagon. "Ain't no trouble."

Jack turned to Eli and the others. "It's not just luck that we made it out okay," he said. "I think it means something."

"It's a sign," Frances said. "A sign that we should all five stay together."

Alexander agreed. "Let's shake hands on it. Swear on it or something."

Jack started to shake Eli's hand, but Eli just held it and Frances' hand, too. One after another they joined their hands in a tight little circle right there in the wagon, just for a moment in the long morning sunlight.

Clement Bay let them ride all the way to Bremerton. He stopped at the depot, where the five children climbed down by the railroad tracks that they would follow on foot.

"Which way y'all headed?" Clement asked them.

"North," Alexander replied.

"Anyone expecting ya up thataways?"

Frances grinned. "You could say that."

Jack looked out at the train tracks and the way they vanished between two green hills. They'd decided it would be too risky to hop a train—too many folks who'd take notice of five waifs on their own, and who knew how many of them were like Miss DeHaven? Besides, now that they'd gotten a ride in the wagon, it was less than ten miles—half a day's walk—to their first destination. Jack studied the horizon again and realized he knew, for the first time, how it felt to be excited about the road ahead.

After one last wave goodbye to Clement, the five of them set off.

As they walked, they passed the time telling Eli stories about the first Wanderville in Kansas, including the time they'd thrown dozens of roasted potatoes at Rutherford Pratcherd.

They sang the Big Rock Candy Mountain song. Then Harold taught them the Cold Water Army song, which they all agreed was not nearly as good a song to sing. In fact, Alexander pointed out, it just made them wish there was colder water in the big glass jar they'd brought along.

The sun got higher in the sky. They stopped to eat lunch in the shade of a big tree, and then they continued on, walking, talking, and singing.

They wondered about Miss DeHaven, too— where she was now and whether she'd even return to the Careys' looking for them.

"Do you think Reverend and Mrs. Carey will keep their promise not to tell her where we went?" Frances asked.

"I don't know," Jack said. "But it's better to be careful if we ever send letters to their farm."

"We could give our letters to a hobo," Alexander suggested. "And ask him to stop off in some town where we've never been and mail them from the post office there."

"That sure would throw Miss DeHaven off our trail," Jack said.

"Speaking of hoboes," Frances said, "we're almost there."

They had come to the edge of another small town, where ahead of them stood the little train depot and its wooden platforms.

"What are you talking about?" Eli asked.

Jack looked over at Frances, who reached into her pocket and took out her reader. It fell open right to the page with the instructions she'd written down.

"We're now in Sherwood, Missouri," Frances announced. "Where our good hobo friend A-Number-One Nickel Ned Handsome left a secret treasure. And we intend to find it."

31

EVERY STEP HAS ITS OWN PRESIDENT

"We've already got the first clue," Frances said, pointing to the cobbler shop sign across the street from the depot—the big wooden boot that hung over the shop door. "'You'll have your boot on in the right direction,'" she read out loud.

Jack nodded. "So we'll go that way?" he asked, pointing east, where the boot's toe was facing. Seemed simple enough, he thought. Maybe too simple.

"Yes," Frances said. "But it's this next one that has me stumped: 'Cross an Indian, a saint, and one of our founding fathers.'"

"Huh," Alexander muttered as they headed down the street to a corner where the storefronts ended and the houses began. They stood there a moment, glancing around.

Then Jack looked over at the street name, which was painted on the side of a post: HIAWATHA.

"I got it! It means cross Hiawatha Street!" he exclaimed. "An Indian!"

"I think you're right!" Frances said, as they all ran across the street. "What's this next street? A saint's name?"

Sure enough, the street post said ST. LOUIS, and they kept going. The street after that was FRANKLIN.

"A founding father," Alexander pointed out.

Frances looked down at her book. "Now I think we turn right. But then it says, 'Just keep going until you get mush.' What does *that* mean?"

"Let's keep going and find out," Eli said.

They all walked three blocks, then four, until they found themselves near the far edge of town. *What if there's nothing here?* Jack wondered. The street had only a row of deserted-looking brick warehouses.

Then Harold yelled, "I see it! Look up!"

They all looked up at the side of one of the warehouses, where painted in fading colors on the brick was an advertisement:

EAT

McCANN'S

MUSH

OAT CEREAL 3 FLAVORS

"*MUSH!*" they all shouted joyfully. It was the best billboard Jack had ever seen for a food he didn't want to try in the slightest.

From there, it wasn't too hard to find the "house with blue eyes that are always shut and has broken teeth." Frances was right that the "blue eyes" were painted shutters; the "broken teeth" were missing rail posts on the front porch.

They went to the edge of the woods, where the space between two big trees seemed to form a sort of doorway.

"'Then count steps,'" Frances read aloud. "'Every step has its own president.'"

Jack took one step, which got him just past the trees. "George Washington," he said. What was the second step? "Thomas Jefferson?"

Frances shook her head. "John Adams. *Then* Jefferson."

She led the step-counting through the woods. "Madison, Monroe . . ." But once she got as far as Lincoln, she hesitated.

"Johnson," Eli said, taking a step. "Grant. Hayes, Garfield, Arthur . . ." He made four more steps.

"I thought you said you stopped going to school!" Jack said.

Eli shrugged. "Just 'cause I can't read so good doesn't mean I can't memorize a bunch of presidents," he said. "Drat! Now I lost my place. Where was I?"

"I see it!" Frances shrieked. "'Once you get to Harrison, check the ground, and you should be on the right track.'"

"What do you see?" Jack said, scanning the dirt and twigs beneath his feet.

And then he saw it, too—steel railroad tracks! A single railroad spur that went through the woods.

They looked to the right and realized the tracks led to a tiny shed of gray weathered wood that blended in so well with the forest surroundings that they hadn't noticed it until now.

The door wasn't locked, and despite the rusty hinges, it opened quite easily.

"There's a note!" Alexander cried, picking it up.

Dear Orphans, it read, in surprisingly elegant script.

> Ned Handsome here. Was just passing through and thought I'd make sure that my treasure is still in good working order. These here train tracks are a side road that you can take west halfway to Oklahoma from here. Hope you got strong arms.
>
> Sincerely, A 1 (5¢) Ned Handsome
>
> PS Tin Whistle and Enzo send their regards.

"Wow," Frances said.

Jack breathed a sigh of relief. "Quentin and Lorenzo—they're all right, wherever they are."

"They're in good company," Alexander agreed. "But now . . . what's in the shed?"

Jack was dying to know, too. He opened the door wider, and the sunlight hit a set of iron handles. Two handles, actually—one at either end of a long arm that was perched on top of a wheeled contraption.

"What is it?" Jack wondered.

"A handcar!" Harold shouted. "I once saw one in a book!"

Frances nodded. "I read you that book!"

"I've heard of these handcar contraptions," Alexander said, stepping inside the shed to get closer. A wooden platform stood atop the wheels, and Alexander climbed up. "It's a little car that moves on train tracks."

Jack jumped up next to Alexander, amazed, followed by Frances and Harold. "How does it work?"

Harold reached up. "You pump the handles up and down! You take turns, like a seesaw!" He pulled down one handle. Then Jack reached out and pulled down the opposite handle. *Up, down*, the long arm went, and the handcar started to move.

"Whoa!" Frances exclaimed. "Eli, jump on!"

The five of them stood on the platform, and Jack and Alexander manned the two handles and began to work the pumping mechanism.

"We've got to make sure we're both strong enough," Alexander said. "But also that we don't overpower each other. Got it?"

"No problem," Jack said, and he meant it.

"We can help, too, you know," Frances said, putting her hands on the handle on Jack's side. Eli did the same on Alexander's, and Harold just held on in the middle.

The car lurched at first and moved slowly, with

a few sharp squeaks from the wheels. But then it began to go more smoothly and pick up speed.

Frances and Harold were laughing and whooping in the new breeze of the handcar's motion. Alexander and Eli were on the side facing backward, so they couldn't see the road in front of them. But they grinned together, side by side, and Jack realized how lucky he was to have all of them as friends.

"You're the one facing forward, Jack," Alexander asked. "Are we going in the right direction?"

Jack could see the afternoon sun ahead of him, right behind his friends.

"We sure are," he said. "We're going west."

ACKNOWLEDGMENTS

Many, many thanks to my amazing editor, Gillian Levinson, as well as the rest of the team at Razorbill: Ben Schrank, Christine Ma, and Theresa Evangelista. I'm grateful as well for the wonderful folks at Penguin, including Kathryn Bhirud, Scottie Bowditch, Sheila Hennessey, and Geoffrey Kloske, and for my agent, Sarah Burnes, for all they've done to support the Wanderville books. And thank you, Erwin Madrid, for bringing Jack, Frances, Harold, and Alexander to life!

To my family and friends—my husband, Chris, Michael Taeckens, Jami Attenberg, and the Gorgeous Ladies of Writing, thank you, too. And a great big trainload of thank-yous to all the terrific kids, teachers, librarians, parents, and booksellers that I've met since book 1 was published, whose comments, questions, and enthusiasm continue to inspire me.

Turn the page to see
where the citizens of

travel next in . . .

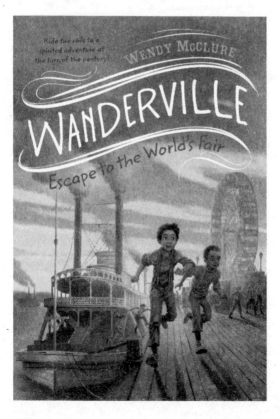

1
A RUN-IN WITH FATE

Down, Jack thought as he pulled the handle. *Down.* He pulled again. *Down.*

The great iron arm creaked and every so often the wheels would scrape as they slid along the tracks. Sometimes the scraping noise was so sharp Jack could hear it with his teeth. But it meant that they were making the handcar go as fast as it could— enough speed for a breeze that turned Frances's hair wild and nearly blew Alexander's cap away—and that was worth it. Even if all five of them wound up bone tired by nightfall again, at least they were going somewhere, right?

As far as Jack could tell, they were in Missouri still—the rusty stretch of railroad track they were on went past quiet cornfields and meadows. Twice they'd seen people—once, when they went by a farmhouse yard where a woman tended a clothesline, and then later, when they passed a man with a horse and plow. Frances's little brother, Harold, had called out hello to them and waved, but the woman had only stared back in amazement and the man had scratched his head. Jack figured it had been years and years since a train had traveled on these tracks, much less a handcar with five kids on board.

The fewer folks they saw, though, the better. They had a long way to travel, after all. Jack had been thinking about it all morning and he was sure the others were, too. *California!* He couldn't believe they were on their way. But then he'd watch the big iron arm on the handcar go up and down like a seesaw and wonder how many times he'd have to pump those handles before they got to California.

Down. Jack pulled again and shifted his weight on his aching feet. Today he was riding backward. When they'd first found the handcar two days ago, Jack and Frances took the side that faced forward, while Alexander and Eli had been on the other side. Sometimes they all switched places, and while it hadn't taken Jack long to get used to the motion of riding that way, he hated that the only thing he could see were the trees and fields behind their vehicle, slipping away into the distance.

"What's . . . ahead?" he managed to ask between deep breaths. "What . . . can . . . you see?"

Eli, who, along with Alexander, had the proper view, shook his head. "Nothin'," he puffed as he pulled down the handles on his end. "Same old . . . thing . . . Fields and stuff."

Harold piped up. "That ain't nothing!" He rode in the middle and held on to their supplies since he was seven and too young to work the handles on the handcar. "I see a big tree, and a barn way over there. . . ."

"*Isn't*," Frances corrected him. She was pulling right next to Jack, but she still had to be the big sister. "Not . . . ain't."

Jack had a feeling it was going to be another long day. Yesterday they'd kept the handcar going well after dusk, until they were so exhausted they could barely speak. They'd stumbled off the tracks and fell onto the nearest bit of grass they could find. Jack's arms had felt sore to the bones, Frances complained of blisters, and Eli had declared that working the handcar was tougher than plowing.

"Just wait," Alexander had said last night,

while they all stretched out in the prickly prairie grass trying to find comfortable spots for sleeping. "Next thing you know, we'll be eating oranges out west. . . ."

His had voice trailed off. Nobody else had spoken; they hadn't the energy to reply.

Jack was glad the five of them were on their own now, and not back at Reverend Carey's farm. Or, worse, still on an orphan train or breaking their backs at the ranch in Kansas. They were free, which meant that they *had* to be better off now.

That's what he kept telling himself, at least. *We're lucky.* He'd say it in his head all day long today if he had to. In between pulling the handle, that is. *Down . . . down.* He knew there were other kids who weren't so lucky.

An hour or so passed, and then another rusty shriek from the handcar wheels snapped Jack out of his thoughts. The awful sound grew louder and Jack could feel himself cringing.

"Ow!" Harold cried, his voice barely carrying above the noise. *"Ow!"*

"What?" Frances called back to her brother. "What is it?"

Harold's eyes were wide as he looked past Jack

and Frances to the tracks ahead. And suddenly Jack realized what Harold was saying. Not *ow* but *look out*!

"We have to stop—" Alexander began. He and Eli could see whatever was ahead too, and they had quit working the handle.

"We have to *brake*!" Eli cut in. "Where's the brake?"

"Here!" Frances reached for it, an iron lever near her feet. She yanked on it with both hands.

The handcar screeched and slowed just enough for Jack to turn around and see the tracks ahead.

Or rather, what was *left* of the tracks.

Where's the bridge? Frances's mouth went dry when she turned and spotted the creek ahead. Where there should have been a bridge, the tracks instead ended in two bent pieces that reached over the high bluff of the creek bank.

"We have to get off this thing!" Jack cried.

The handcar was still going plenty fast, its brake noise shrill and awful. The bank was just a few yards away and coming closer. Frances reached across to grab Harold's sleeve, getting ready to pull him along into a well-timed jump—

But with a bump and a *BANG!*, the handcar

slammed to a sudden stop. Frances lost her footing and toppled off one side, dragging Harold with her.

"Oooof!" She hit the ground hard on her backside.

Alexander stumbled over and offered her a hand. "You all right?"

Frances nodded and got up. She looked around: Her brother had managed to land on his feet, though he'd dropped the floursack full of supplies. Jack and Eli had gone off the other side of the handcar, and they were slowly pulling themselves off the ground.

"What just happened?" she murmured.

"It's broken!" Harold cried, pointing over to where the handcar stood tilted to one side like a collapsed table. "The wheels came off the track!"

"Looks like it derailed," Alexander said. He showed Frances and the others a spot along the tracks where two lengths of rail had come apart.

Frances looked over by the creek where the tracks abruptly ended. The bridge must have fallen long ago and the rails on the bank had buckled. She was glad that the handcar hadn't just pitched them all straight into the rocky creek bed, but now that it had gone off the rails it was useless. She watched as Jack kicked the handcar wheels, his jaw set. He reached up and yanked the big iron arm, which made a feeble creak.

"Forget it," Eli said to Jack. "That thing isn't going anywhere."

Frances knew Eli was right. Even if they could fix it, there was no way they could haul it across the creek to where the tracks continued. She stepped closer to the wreck and sighed when she saw the snapped cables and a big splintery crack down one side of the platform.

"That was our treasure," she said softly.

I'm sorry, Ned Handsome, she thought to herself. Ned was a hobo they'd met while riding the rails out of Kansas. Before they'd parted ways, he'd given them a mysterious set of directions leading to a "treasure" he'd stashed away. For weeks Frances had puzzled over the clues and dreamed of finding it.

And she had; she'd found the handcar. Over the past two days they'd used it to travel more than sixty miles all by themselves. It had seemed like there'd be no stopping them. *Until now.*

Frances had to bite her lip to keep back the tears. She glanced up to see Alexander looking over solemnly, as if to say he was sorry too. It helped to know that he understood.

Harold came over to her side and squeezed her hand. "Don't be sad, Frannie. Nobody got hurt too bad."

She squeezed his hand back. "You're right. We're lucky." She was glad for the reminder. It could have been much worse. But Harold had nothing more than a couple of dirty scuffs on his knickers, Frances and Alexander had just a few scrapes and bruises, and Eli had a skinned knee that he was washing in the creek. As for Jack, he seemed unhurt, but his shoulders slumped and he rubbed his eyes like he had a terrible headache.

"What do we do now?" Jack asked, looking around at all of them. "How are we ever going to get to California?"

Nobody answered for a moment. But Frances turned to look at Alexander. She had a feeling he'd have something to say.

"That's a good question, Jack," he said. "But for now, we start by walking."